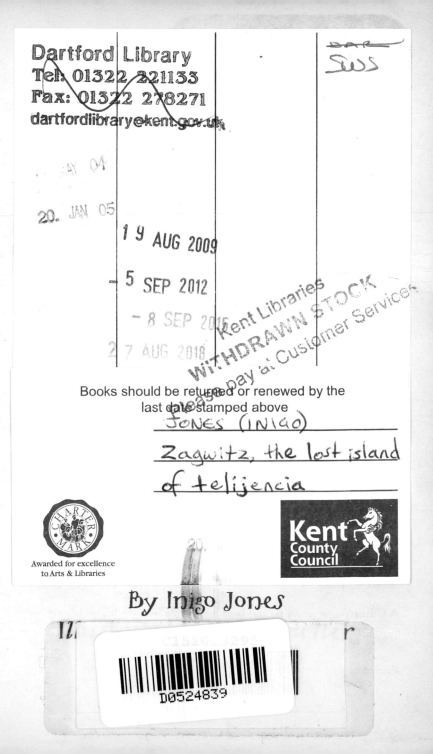

Books should be returned or renewed by the
last date stamped above

JONES (INIGO)

Zagwitz, the lost island
of telijencia

By Inigo Jones

SIMON &
SCHUSTER

First published in Great Britain by Simon & Schuster UK Ltd, 2002
A Viacom Company

3 5 7 9 10 8 6 4 2

Simon and Schuster UK Ltd
Africa House
64-78 Kingsway
London WC2B 6AH

Simon & Schuster
Australia Sydney

A CIP catalogue record for this book is available from the British Library

ISBN 0 689 836856

Printed by Cox & Wyman Ltd, Reading

In memory of my dear mum who always
enjoyed a really good chuckle,
and if she could read this book would still
think I was as daft as a brush.

– D.P.J.

Contents

Gudorphal

Somewhere in a dank, pulsating, gooey cavern deep within Lurkamungoo, the putrid hub of nothingness, an odd, damp, squidgy warmth and a series of stiff prods began to wake Eraser. Feeling snug, as if lying on a waterbed, he expelled a series of booming snorts reminiscent of a foghorn with severe constipation.

Life had been a real drag for Eraser since he had crashed his flying Camcracraft into the ocean and sunk down to the murky depths, when trying to escape from Astral and Zag. Strong underwater currents had continuously bashed him and his stingray-shaped machine into reefs and wrecks. The irony was complete. This evil craft, which he'd used to terrorise the Rutilan inhabitants on the Island of Blot by whisking them away into its flashgun, had become his prison.

Whereas Eraser's adversary, Astral, had been promoted to Defender General and Protector of the Galaxy of Ideas, a just reward for his bravery in working undercover as 'Artless the Heartless', Eraser's second-in-command.

However, it had taken more than Astral's heroism to bring about the downfall of Eraser the Terrible. A meddlesome seagull had also made an inadvertent contribution which ultimately provided Astral with crucial help in the form of Zagwitz, the twins Lucy and William, and the owl, Awoo. Ever since that adventure, Eraser had lain sparked-out and hopelessly trapped inside his craft.

Until, like muck flushed down a sewer, the Cameracraft had been sucked through a vortex of water and whooshed into Lurkamungoo. The whole cavernous mire was encapsulated in an ooze-pulsating membrane. Festering honeycomb-shaped cavities spurted odorous pongs that stank like mouldy cabbage-juice mixed with decaying fish guts. Larger vents offered gunge-dripping access into murky passageways. The conical roof held a sinister chandelier of what appeared to be giant balloons all clustered together like a huge mouldy bunch of grapes. Some glowed and their luminous green shimmer lit up the dank cavern, others were slightly faded – but most had dimmed down to a murky pale-brown as if their bulbs had blown.

Eraser was soon to find out all about the awful secrets of Lurkamungoo – especially the Globolloons.

Dozens of slimy creatures, with translucent membranous sac-bodies the size of dustbins, smothered his craft. The fat, ugly torsos tapered forward to form a socket, holding two puce-orange eyes which sat gawkily side by side. Attached almost spider-like around their bodies, each beast had six sucker-footed tentacles which it used to relentlessly thump, tug and pound the Cameracraft. These were the Lurkwarriors, fiendish servants to the Rulers of Lurkamungoo.

At first it was the large telescopic lens

protruding from its tapered nose, and the broad, silvery, diamond-shaped window inset into its brow, that drew their frenzied attack. This held the powerful flashlight of the one-time flying Cameracraft which, in its dreadful heyday, took photographs that not only stole the images of its victims but also captured their very beings.

Suddenly the Cameracraft's canopy yielded. The Lurkwarriors' repulsive squirming bodies undulated yellow and green with excitement at the sight of Eraser lying exposed and unconscious in his cockpit. Then suddenly, a loud, snorting spittle-bellow resounded about the cavern, making them scurry into nearby vibrating cavities like rabbits dashing for cover into a warren. But don't be fooled! These fiends were afraid of nothing bar the wrath of the masters for whom they had been bred to serve at all costs.

A dominant and much larger, blubbery, slug-like creature, wearing a hooded shroud made of membrane, slithered swiftly towards the craft. Looking like a wrinkled walrus smacked full in the mouth by an errant ship's rudder, its ghastly pug-face had lips like a distorted sink-plunger. Two tentacular arms unfolded grotesquely away from its body, as did a thinner third arm centred on its forehead. Each limb had three sucker-fingers which in unison clamped onto Eraser then yanked him out of the craft and unceremoniously dumped him into an unspeakable mess of gooey green mucus. The hideous creature touched its snoring victim with its retractable forehead-tentacle: inspecting, sniffing, slobbering. With a swish of its slithery tail, it gob-spittled angrily as two more of its kind flew in on slithersticks two metres long and twice as thick as a broom-handle, with a bulbous knob at the rear end and a flared trumpet-like bell at the front.

"Malodour! You is supposed to be me Keeper of the Lurkwarriors!" splurted the larger of the two, landing upright beside the creature. He looked like a huge wobbly abscess stuck to a flagpole. Emitting a greasy-yellow lubricating foam, he slid down his slitherstick. "Ya'snot replacing Mucid as me Slime Minister unless you is finding me that thieving git AND getting me Festalpod back!" Gudorphal bellowed furiously.

Malodour slithered away, ashamed, seething and determined to put matters right. The Lurkwarriors had not only failed him, one of the privileged few destined to be a leader of a new colony but, even worse, they had failed their ruler.

"If you is not moving more bluntish, I'll downgriddle you to a Lurkwarrior!" Gudorphal continued to slobber-shout at him.

"You's being bullyaching bumptious at him," slurped Putridia, sliding off her slitherstick and prodding the snoring Eraser with it. "S'not his fault the Lurklouts keeps going missling!"

"Lurklouts grows up to be Lurkwarriors," Gudorphal spittled angrily.

"Yooze let Mucid go hatchling more with

your Festalpod!" Putridia splurted, "I warned yas'not to." Seeing Eraser twitch, she gave him a few extra hard pokes.

"WHAT THE HECK IS...?" Eraser yelled, suddenly sitting bolt upright to find himself soaking in a pool of lukewarm, viscous, dark-green, smelly slime, confronted by two repulsive bog-eyed creatures who seemed to have horrendous runny colds of galactic proportions.

"Its mouth's running," mucus-dripped Putridia.

"KEEP AWAY FROM ME!" Eraser yelled, appalled at the goo-ridden cavern spewing obnoxious bubbles. Fumbling inside his soggy pocket he found his pomander and sniffed the sodden bag. No longer fragrant with pleasant aromatic substances, the experience was far more devastating than the first lick of salt when you thought it was sugar. "UUGGHEEE!" he heaved, "THIS STINKS LIKE YOU!"

"Anything true nastable stinks!" splurted Putridia.

Eraser slopped about, furious at the sight of his ruined pirate finery. Torn ruffles dangled from his clingy, faded-orange silk shirt. His long purple dress-coat hung, gunk-stained and ripped, across his scrawny shoulders. "I'VE ALWAYS BEEN NASTY!" he hollered, unravelling his dripping coat-tails, "AND I DIDN'T STINK!"

"S'not true nastable then," Gudorphal slurped casually at Putridia, who was still giving Eraser the occasional dig.

"WILL YOU STOP PRODDING ME!" Eraser yelled, discovering only half of his high lapels remained and removed the other half, which had stuck in his mop of matted, frizzy ginger hair. "IN FACT I'M POSITIVELY EVIL!" he bawled, "SO DON'T MESS WITH ME!" Eraser floundered in the slime trying desperately to stand up and regain his dignity. "AND YOU'RE A RIGHT PAIR OF UGLY, REPULSIVE OOZE-BAGS!"

"Compliments, too!" Putridia pushed aside her membrane hood and flicked her sinewy tendrilous hair as if posing for a photograph. To her, ugly was beautiful, repulsive was heavenly, and being both to the utmost extreme, she thought she was gorgeous. "Yooze far too nice."

"Nice! ME... NICE?" Eraser's piggy eyes bulged with fury, as he managed to upright himself precariously. "I'm terrible! I AM ERASER."

"A rasher?" Gudorphal interrupted contemptuously.

Putridia bog-eyed into Eraser's face and slobber-smirked. "Snores like a pig, has eyes like a pig and a mug like a skinny pig's bum!"

The large boil on the end of Eraser's long nose pulsated to bursting point. "NOW LISTEN HERE, BOG-BREATH..."

"Putridia the Putrishan!" she retorted. "He's Gudorphal the Downright, Presidumpt of Lurkamungoo."

The mention of his title reawakened Gudorphal's concern about Malodour retrieving his Festalpod. He needed it badly to accomplish his rotten ambitions and create more legions of Lurkwarriors. The tentacle unfolded out of his forehead, slid down his face and across his fat lips. Wiping away a wad of oozing saliva, he exposed his gummy-green, toothless orifice and splurted, "Enough of yours drivel! You is about to be history!"

"Oh yeah!" Eraser scoffed. "What'ya going to do, BITE ME?"

"No, Mister Streaky," Gudorphal slurped nonchalantly, "I'm going to globollise you!"

"Globollise ME?" Eraser gulped, having no clue what it meant except it sounded truly nasty.

"Pity, I prefer globollising kiddybeens," said Putridia.

"KIDNEY BEANS?"

"No!" spittled Gudorphal, impatiently, "KIDS! Those things that Beingsh call children."

"Oh good, that's all right then!" Eraser heaved a sickly grin, "Cos I hate KIDS, they're useless!"

"No they is not! They pusitively oozle

with energy and make spanking good putricity too." Putridia inspected the lanky mess that had been sucked into Lurkamungoo. "The only thing oozling's your boil, you is so widdly."

"WIDDLY!" Eraser bawled, "WHAT'YA THINK YOU ARE?"

"POLLUTICIANS," spat Gudorphal, proudly, "RULERS OF THE LURKS AND LURKAMUNGOO!"

"AND the Cesspitial Galaxy of Incognito," Putridia added. "And alls-over everywhere else we're going to rule and putrify."

"Wait, wait, wait, wait, WAIT!" said Eraser, excitedly. "Now you're talking my language."

Gudorphal folded two of his tentacles onto his gut. "Oh, is that so?"

"Yes, yes, yes, yes, YES!" Eraser rubbed his greasy hands and gave an encouraging smile. "Rule... PETRIFY... I'm ace at all that sort of thing!"

"PUTRIFY!" splattered Putridia. "Not

petrify, yooze nurd!"

"DON'T CALL ME A..." Eraser thought better of arguing. "It's all tantamount to the same thing," he said gleefully, "I should know, I am an expert at it all!"

"We dribbles the same language, eh?" Gudorphal spittled. "Then how's you is spilling 'putrify'?"

Eraser looked simply smug. "P U T R E F Y."

"WRONG!" Gudorphal looked even more smug. "Putridia, you is the Putrician, spill out the difference."

Teacher-like, Putridia stuck a thoughtful sucker under her quadruple chin and began to recite her short lecture in spelling.

"**Petrify**... spilled with **E** and **I** is what we will dooze to make you cry.

"**Putrefy**... spilled with a **U** and **E** happens when yooze no longer be.

"**Putrify**... spilled with **U** and **I** is what we dooze to drain you to fly."

For a moment Eraser looked confused. "Oh... Train me to fly?" The penny-dropped.

"Oh... that's okay then... No need... I'm an expert at that too."

"DRAIN NOT TRAIN!" Gudorphal spluttered in exasperation. "Explain to Pigglywiddly
for the very last time, Putridia!"

Baffled and anxious to learn his fate, Eraser ignored the insult and listened intently to the bad news.

Putridia gob-eyed Eraser's concentration and duly informed him of the process. "We puts yooze inside a Globolloon, drains yooze energy, then pop it into a Putrisphere to make putricity currents to fuel our slither-sticks."

"And you is not knowing half of it," Gudorphal slobbered.

"W...what does that mean?" gasped Eraser.

"It means you is going on a one-way crooze to Globscurity!" splurted Gudorphal.

"Rotten shame," Putridia slobber-cackled. "BYEZEE BYE-BYES!"

"GLOBSCURITY?" Eraser cried out, all

of a tremble.

"Globscurity is the place you is going after you is been dimmed of life and you is not mattering no more," said Gudorphal casually, pointing his slitherstick at Eraser. Eraser started to run for it, slipped headlong, slid nose-boil first into the side of his wrecked Cameracraft and hollered painfully.

"Ya'snot going to feel the slightest thing," Putridia dribbled, "so calm down."

"Not feel a thing! CALM down she says!" Eraser twitched like a flea-bitten rat. "I'VE NEVER CALMED DOWN IN MY LIFE!"

"Ya'swill now," gobble-spat Gudorphal menacingly. The slitherstick's flared, trumpet-like end glowed and out of it grew a ghastly snot-green bubble.

Slipping, sliding and scrambling, Eraser desperately tried to make his escape across the cavernous mire towards a flapping vent, but the massive bubble bounced after him, quickly enveloping its prey. He tried manically to break out by stretching the translucent, rubbery slime-wall with violent punches and kicks. His vigorous efforts proved worthless as he floated upwards to join the Globolloons that were clustered together like a chandelier of balloons in the conical roof. The more Eraser struggled, the brighter the luminous green of his bubble glowed, casting even more shadows in the dank cavern. Already the other Globolloons were fading to a pale murky-brown of insignificance.

"Widdly's oozing much bitter than I inspected," Putridia remarked, listening to the muffled yells as they waited for Malodour to return with Mucid. "I'll globollise Mucid foremost then putrify them both to Globscurity."

"Need oozles more putricity than that!" Gudorphal splurted thoughtfully.

Lurkamungoo was an ecological nightmare created by his Festalpod, a knobbly, chrysalis-shaped object the length of a baseball bat. Gudorphal's lurid ambitions meant there was nothing he wouldn't do to recover the Festalpod and bring a plague of devastation to every world – and this was only the beginning!

The Intrusion

Worlds apart, a small lean-to conservatory – Zag's Thinking-Pad attached to the side of his rickety barn – glowed with excitement. Zag had been writing out a calculation, when suddenly his sheet of note-paper burst into a fizz of brilliant colours, turned into silky-smooth parchment and official writing appeared. Crowding around his home-made desk, Lucy and William were ecstatic, Zag amazed, Awoo hoot-struck and Flewy beak-smacked. Nobody could have wished for anything better! It was the twins' last night at Zag's house and at the precise moment they were feeling sad about their weekend stay coming to an end – it all happened! Not that Zag had planned it this way, but the timing was rather perfect.

His Eminence the Master of Creativity

Hereby gives notice that he wishes to bestow

THE ORDER OF INGENUITY

upon

Zagwitz the Thingummagadgetician

and thereby appoint him

FELLOW OF THE GALACTIC CIRCLE

For his outstanding courage in recovering The Orb of Brilliance

and protecting The World of Creativity and The Galaxy of Ideas

And award

THE FREEDOM of THE ISLAND of RADIANCE

to

Lucy and William the Twins, and to Twit-Awoo the Owl

In recognition of their unselfish support and friendship to the cause

PS. Tried vista-mail but your Cosmoputa's
not registered on the Infinet.
See you on the Island of Radiance soon
for dinner aboard the good ship Mobsea
Dick!!! Your grateful friend, Astral

The air buzzed with individual
recollections of their fight against Eraser –

his terrible rule over the island which he'd plunged into darkness and named *'Blot'* – their first meeting with Eggbert the Eagle, bereft at the loss of his mate Eggna and living forlorn and alone in his smelly cave – how they hid from the Cameracraft – how the awesome Mogster-pirates, at first fierce enemies, became friends and helped them defeat Eraser and transform 'Blot' into the beautiful tropical Island of Radiance.

It was at the mention of the Mogsters that Awoo's keen eyes noticed something very unsavoury. He scrambled across the desk and picked up the parchment, which showered colourful sparks as he pointedly tapped it with his other wing. "Dinner on the good ship *Mobsea Dick*!" he hooted, aghast, reading the postscript out loud. "That galleon is rancid!"

Zag puffed out his cheeks, hardly believing it himself, and stretched his sleeveless yellow waistcoat with a thumb in each armhole. "Seems that's where we've been invited to receive the awards."

"Let me see!" squawked Flewy, barging into the owl and trying to snatch the parchment from him.

"Doesn't affect you," said Awoo. Keeping it out of Flewy's reach, he handed it to Zag for safe-keeping. "You seagulls are all scavengers, which I guess is also indicative of your bad manners."

Flewy put his wings on his hips and stamped indignantly on the desk with his webbed foot. "I'll have you know I take great pride in my diet!"

"Pity that doesn't apply more often to your behaviour," Zag scolded, as he began to read the parchment more closely.

"I wonder if the Mogsters have turned it into a floating restaurant," said Lucy, gathering her dark hair into a ponytail and twisting it back inside the rubberband.

"Bet Gutrumble's the head chef!" Flewy squawked, whilst poking a wing towards his beak, making a sick gesture.

William smiled mischievously at his sister. "Yeah, cooking with all those rotting rats hanging around his fat gut."

Like the colour of their hair, the grins that the twins exchanged were near identical.

"And squishy rats-eyes popping out into the food," Lucy giggled impishly, adding to the mental picture.

"If that is the case, I'll observe while you chaps eat," Awoo hooted. "God only knows what would be on the menu."

"Even God wouldn't want to know that," chuckled Zag, his kindly blue eyes looking up from the parchment. "At least the *Mobsea Dick* stayed afloat."

"That's a wonder in itself," said Awoo, having had a feather-raising experience when sailing with the Mogsters on the *Mobsea Dick*, "considering they're even more daft than they look."

"They wanted to eat me once!" squawked Flewy, trying to get some attention as the rest laughed about the Mogsters' pirate-gangster clothes: the low-slung trilby hats, pin-striped suit jackets at odds with their tights and swashbuckling boots, and the way they carried their cutlasses in violin cases.

"Now that would have been daft," Awoo twittered with laughter, "they could have been poisoned."

"Wasn't funny!" Flewy squawked, reminded of his first horrifying encounter with Ally Catpone, Gutrumble and Spooky, as they prowled the island for Eraser. "I was nearly chopped up by a cutlass... I was abandoned in that cave, nowhere to go, all on my own and..."

"Eraser forced them into that situation," said Lucy, in their defence.

"Not into try eating me, he didn't," Flewy replied.

"Any rate, they're our friends now," said William, not wanting the conversation to turn negative, "and they helped us beat Eraser."

"Especially Legs Diamonté," said Awoo. "She was so brave, I'd never have thought it."

"That's because your brain's too small to think," beaked Flewy.

"I would so like to meet her again," Lucy smiled, thoughtful of the close bond she and William had built up with Legs, and how this sleek, beautiful Mogster's moll, constantly fussing about her looks, had totally disregarded her own safety to save them from Eraser.

The sheet of scrap notepaper which had turned into silky-smooth parchment was still fizzing brilliant colours around its edges as Zag adjusted his half-rimmed glasses. He bit his lip as if to stop himself saying something.

"Mum and Dad won't arrive until the morning," implored William, fast detecting the hesitation.

"Please," pleaded Lucy, "it could be ages before we're all together again."

"True enough." Zag twiddled his bushy white beard thoughtfully. "But I've two problems," he said, making everybody's hearts sink. "I have to complete installing the Cosmoputa in the Beamsurfer."

"Oh great!" squawked Flewy, rudely. "Nothing new about that!"

"It's your inability to fly without a wobble that's caused this!" said Awoo.

"This should only take me half an hour." Zag shook his head. "But..."

"Let's go," said William, not wanting to hear anything following a 'but'.

Neither did Lucy. "We can beamsurf there quickly and..."

"Unless we get lost again, like the last time." Flewy quickly ducked his head under his wing to avoid the killer looks fired in his direction.

"...return the same time as we leave," said Awoo, supportively, having visions of being a guest professor at Harvard, Yale, Oxford, Cambridge and the like. "After all, a very prestigious honour is being bestowed upon us!"

Zag frowned. "There still remains the problem concerning the twins."

"They're too noisy!" quipped Flewy, unable to keep his beak shut.

"US?" cried William. "Huh, you've got a nerve!"

"What is the problem, Zag?" asked Lucy, hoping she could solve it.

"I can't let you stay up any later, it's nearly nine o'clock already."

"Special circumstances," Lucy responded, as quick as a flash.

"And we're still dressed and ready to go," added William, prompting Lucy to briefly check that her pale-blue jeans and dark-blue hooded sweat-top still looked okay. William wasn't bothered about such matters, as proven by the fact that he wore his much-faded denim shirt constantly. Although he did think the rips in the knees of his jeans were 'cool'.

"I must have been teasing," Zag chuckled. However, there was something only he'd noticed during the joviality that he had to tell Flewy. He decided it was best to wait until they boarded the Beamsurfer. "SO! What are we waiting for?"

"Whoopee!" shouted Lucy and William, dancing about with joy.

Zag stood up from behind his desk. Although short in stature, he still couldn't get over how the twins had grown – Lucy was now as tall as him and William even a shade taller.

"Thought your Cosmoputa needed sorting," squawked Flewy, with some uncertainty, having revived his own scary memories of the last adventure.

"I'll do that now," said Zag, "that's if I can find enough room to move. Lucy, you help me. William can fetch whatever you both need for the trip." Handing Flewy a small, red helmet with goggles and a small, shiny fin with straps wrapped around it, he said, "This Antiwobble-finthruster is your responsibility." Zag lifted his fez and scratched his head, amazed that he'd actually said that to Flewy of all seagulls. "Oh, and Awoo..."

"I'll sort myself out, thank you!" the owl replied indignantly, considering himself to be the most organised out of the lot of them by far. "And you're going to look a right idiot if you wear that!" he hooted at Flewy as they left.

"At least I'm making the effort," Flewy screeched. "You're only jealous because I'll be able to fly better and faster than you!"

"I think we'll leave them to sort themselves out," Zag muttered to Lucy. One after the other he passed her plans of Thingummagadgets to put onto his homemade desk.

"Portable Folding Car Park to confuse traffic wardens," she giggled, reading the labels. "Citrus Cuddler?"

"Lets a sad lemon give itself a squeeze," replied Zag, getting covered in cobwebs.

"A Bedside Limp?" she continued, as more files hit the cluttered desk.

Zag was more concerned about finding the instructions. "Helps you hop into bed." He peered over his glasses. "Where you and William should be."

"You're really going to make these?" she asked, not having taken the hint.

"Maybe," he smiled, relieved to find the instructions caught in a paper-clip attached to plans for a Bulldozer which sent cattle to sleep. Considering the disorganised chaos of Zag's Thinking Pad, it was amazing how quickly he found his small box of Cosmoputa components.

"I must clean this place up a bit sometime," muttered Zag, brushing the dust off his red trousers with his hands. He put on his bright blue Thingummajacket, full of daft but sometimes useful Thingummagadgets, he and Lucy hurried through the huge, open wooden doors into the main barn.

As always, Zag stopped for a second to admire his Beamsurfer before he climbed aboard proudly. Some of Zag's Thingumma-gadgets were in fact very clever and the Beamsurfer was a brilliant example of his genius. It looked like a sleek rotorless helicopter sitting upon two frisbees, which in turn were placed on top of a silver surf-board. At the end of its long, thin tail was a shiny star.

Since helping Astral fight Eraser, Zag had fitted the Beamsurfer with some very clever modifications. These included the Cosmoputa, more sophisticated than any computer invented. Zag had designed it to tap into the beampower systems. Its built-in Multi Unit Sensor Exponent, his processor, was unlimited by current knowledge and, when linked to a Fibrostatic Sensor Root, could search and decipher the energy carried in electromagnetic lightwaves and interpret the wonders of the universe. Eventually, he hoped it would take the Beamsurfer into Cyber-space, which was what he was working on when his notepaper started glowing and turned into a silky-smooth parchment.

"Everything we need, I think," puffed William, lugging a bulging suitcase.

"Put it down," Zag grinned, shaking his head. "What are those birds up to?" he asked, letting the twins climb aboard and handing the small box of Cosmoputa components to Lucy.

"Arguing whether Flewy'll be too scared to fly in the dark," laughed William.

"And?" asked Lucy, as Zag rummaged in the box.

"He says he's not," William answered, "and wants Zag to make sure he's wearing his Antiwobble-finthruster correctly before he tries it out."

"He'll have to wait," said Zag, checking the contents of the small component box which Lucy held open on her lap. "Right." Zag stroked his beard. "Now let me see," he muttered. "Two sachets of Nebulostic Suspension Gel with NSG Fixing Solution;

a purple Centrifugal Novacrystal complete with MUSE processor; one Fibrostatic Sensor Root; one Astromistical Spray-capsule and three Cosmo-fobs."

The twins watched in awe as Zag assembled the Cosmoputa. "Could you pass the Novacrystal... the purple saucer-sized disc with a hole drilled in it halfway into the middle?"

Lucy carefully handed it to him. It was a few centimetres thick and she was surprised to find it was so light in weight.

"Not as fragile as it looks, stronger than steel. I made it from cosmic particles found only in the Galaxy of Ideas," said Zag, checking to make sure the MUSE processor was in place at the base of the hole. "The particles were a gift from Astral," he added, placing the disc on the flat surface above the instrument panel and setting it firmly in position by tapping it twice with a rubber mallet. "I'll have the sachets next, please."

William handed Zag the sachets. "And the fixing solution?"

"Not quite yet." Zag chuckled at William's impetuosity. "But you can have the Fibrostatic Sensor Root ready for me. It looks like the root of a sapling." Squeezing the two sachets of Nebulostic Suspension Gel into the hole in the Purple Centrifugal Novacrystal he inserted the Fibrostatic Sensor Root. "Fixing Solution, please."

"Seems more like the art of bonsai," said William, handing it to him.

"More botanical than hi-tech," agreed Lucy, watching intently.

"Close," smiled Zag. "It is like planting a miniature tree, but instead of drawing water from earth, the Fibrostatic Sensor Root penetrates far into the ether, searching for and collecting signals which are analysed and developed by the processor I fitted into the Novacrystal." Having made sure the Fibrostatic Sensor Root was 'planted' in the correct position, Zag added in the NSG fixing solution.

Suddenly, like a genie gushing out of a bottle, a spherical holographic silvery mist appeared, soft-lit, and encapsulated in a laser-like network of tinted purpled light.

"W i c k e d!" the twins gasped.

"Done it!" exclaimed Zag, looking as pleased as a cheeky little bear with buckets of honey. "The vista-globe, that's what we needed to see."

"There're still four things left in the box," said Lucy, inquisitively.

"Put them in the compartment next to my seat." Zag was already climbing out to put the twins' suitcase on board. "You'll see what they're for later."

"I'm ready!" hooted Awoo, perching close by the suitcase. "I hope you lot are more organised than..."

"Mumph-mesquawk-mimff!"shrieked Flewy,wearing a skew-whiff red helmet and carrying an unruly bunch of straps in his beak. He waddled furiously across the barn, stood beside Zag and slapped the ground repeatedly with his webbed foot. "Mm fedumpff!"

"Glad to see you're not breaking the habit

of a lifetime," laughed Zag, taking the straps from Flewy's beak. "Stand still and I'll fit it properly."

"Not before time," beaked Flewy, ungraciously. "I'm always left til last!"

Zag straightened the bright-red leather helmet with built-in, flip-down, sensor-light goggles, then attached it to the to adjustable safety release straps.

Flewy lifted his wings. "That tickles," he squawked, as the straps were linked around his body to secure the Antiwobble-finthruster in place. The sleek tail-fin sat along Flewy's back with two astro-lite cylinders, no bigger than fountain-pen tops, positioned each side. These contained extra-long-life self-frictionising jet-propulsion granules, letting him fly like a rocket.

"There, get aboard," said Zag. "Flying with a wobble's a thing of the past."

"I'm SUPERGULL!" screeched Flewy, shoving his way through the cockpit door.

"Will you stop jabbing me!" Awoo hooted, unhappy at having to share a seat with the seagull, as they settled into the Beamsurfer.

"Pardon me for living!" Flewy responded, giving the owl another irritating dig with his tail-fin.

Zag took out the silky-smooth parchment from his Thingummajacket. "Flewy, there has been what I believe to be an error and..."

"The only error I know of is Awoo," beaked Flewy.

Zag continued, "...your name is not mentioned on this award."

Completely beak-smacked, Flewy flipped up his goggles to make certain, carefully read the parchment then gasped, "But why not me?"

"Obvious." Awoo peered pompously down his beak. "It clearly states, *for unselfish support!*"

"He was there as well as us!" said William, giving Awoo a stern look.

"Indeed you were," said Lucy feeling sorry for Flewy. "It must be a mistake... you'll see."

"Which I promise to sort out," said Zag, taking back the parchment.

"I'm always getting left out," said Flewy, purely to gain more sympathy, because he was convinced by his own ego that it had to be a mistake.

"Settle down and fasten your safety-belts," Zag commanded, closing the cockpit door. "World of Creativity... the Island of Radiance, please."

"Can't help you there, sorry," squawked Flewy, cheekily.

"Shush," said Lucy, "Zag's talking to the Cosmoputa."

"Silly question to ask a twit, but do you know what it does?" Flewy asked.

"Hmm." Awoo put on his trying-to-be-wise look. "It's a... it's a whatever it is, and I'll have you remember my name is no longer hyphenated."

"Better tell Astral that because he wrote Twit-Awoo on the parchment," said Flewy. "So he must think you're a real Twit as well!"

"Behave, Flewy, I'm setting co-ordinates

and locking into the beam," Zag scolded, as an image of the island appeared in the vista-globe. "Okay, sit back, relax and enjoy the trip," he said, pressing some buttons. A deep, swishing noise rapidly whirled to a very high pitch, finally becoming barely audible like the soft sound of a distant hairdryer. Zag pulled a lever slowly back to halfway and the Beamsurfer gently lifted one metre off the ground, obediently rotating one hundred and eighty degrees. With a terrific whoosh, it took off through the big open barn doors and surfed the beam into the star-lit night sky.

Awoo took time out to doze and Lucy, William and Flewy chatted amongst them-selves, allowing Zag to monitor the Beamsurfer's progress on the Cosmoputa's vista-globe. He chuckled to himself, wonder-ing who in their right mind would visit a restaurant run by Catpone, a huge panther-like cat with an eye patch and a deep, jagged scar which split his nose and deformed his face. Or be served by a massive slob of a chef like Gutrumble whose gut was not something you'd want close to you at dinner. "But there again," he pondered quietly, "there is Spooky, who always looks dapper, and of course the beautiful Legs Diamonté." Then he remembered the grotty looking state of the rest of the motley ship's crew. "No chance," he smiled happily to himself, as his craft entered the Galaxy of Ideas.

A radiant blue planet appeared on the vista-globe, shining out of the darkness, overwhelming the galaxy with its awesome beauty. It was the World of Creativity, and soon it would be time for him to land.

Gutrumble's Memento!

The glorious sunshine spread a warm golden greeting to the Beamsurfer as it entered the World of Creativity. Awoo hooted a snore as Zag opened the observation window allowing the twins and Flewy to view their approach to the tropical Island of Radiance. Far below them, the sea shimmered varying shades of blue, marking the coral reefs and the deeper parts of the ocean. It all looked so different from Eraser's time, so lush, so green, and so tranquil – like an emerald set into sapphires. The Beamsurfer sped towards the cliffs then a short way inland over a dense area of palm trees, before turning left and back in the direction of the sea.

"LOOK!" Lucy shouted in excitement, startling a dozing Awoo into life.

"W...w...what's h...happening?" Awoo panicked.

Zag was delighted as he landed in a sandy clearing close to a cove; the Cosmoputa had performed a splendid job of navigation.

"It's the *Mobsea Dick*!" shouted William.

Zag slid open the cockpit door. A little way past a thin cluster of palm trees, the Mogster-pirates' galleon could clearly be seen, nestled on its mooring. Unmistakably silver, exactly as they'd last seen it when the island was freed, it glinted in the sun as if twinkling its own deluge of welcomes.

"D'you have to be so noisy?" Awoo blinked his eyes. "For a moment I thought…" he yawned, "I thought we'd…" he yawned again, "I thoug…"

"SEE! Told you!" squawked Flewy. "No brains, can't think!"

"Dressed like a moron, act like a moron, fly like a moron!" retorted Awoo.

"I can out-fly you anytime you choose," boasted Flewy.

"Come on, let's go!" called William excitedly, noticing Zag had finished checking the instrument panel to make sure everything was switched off.

"One last thing to do," said Zag, following everybody out of the craft, then sliding the door shut. He twiddled a silver button on the lapel of his Thingummajacket. The Beamsurfer faded into a ghostly image, like a pencilled drawing on acetate, becoming so transparent that the tropical woods behind could clearly be seen.

He grinned at the surprised faces. "My Thingummagadgetal Chameleoniser. Far more convenient than the invisibilising sheet."

"Cool," said William. "Blends well into the background too."

"Unlike Flewy," giggled Lucy, casting an eye over his Antiwobble-finthruster outfit, complete with tail-fin, bright-red helmet and goggles.

"M'lady," the seagull bowed gallantly, "I'm at your service!" He stuck out his wings to take off, bashed straight into the Beamsurfer, and belatedly fell over to hide his embarrassment.

"You okay, Supergull?" laughed Lucy.

"SUPERDULL would be more appropri-ate," Awoo scoffed.

"As you're so clever, race me to the ship, dim-twit," Flewy challenged.

The twins and Zag made their way down the winding path and onto the harboured cove. Flewy and Awoo remained by the scarcely visible Beamsurfer arguing about which mast on the *Mobsea Dick* was to be the finishing line.

The creaking makeshift pontoon seemed somewhat unstable as they walked towards the galleon. Half-fixed to the gangway was a large blank board, shaped like a big cat's paw with a fingered claw pointing upwards, waiting for a smaller sign to be nailed onto it.

"DAT DUZ IT, I'M OFF! I'VE 'AD A NIFF!" The angry outburst was swiftly followed by a poorly cut sheet of plywood hurled over the side of the ship. The sign caught the breeze and landed just in front of the Zag and the twins.

"Yuh mean *enough*, YUH WIMP! No wonder yuh can't write proper!" bawled a recognisable voice. "Yuh gets wight up my pwitty little nose!"

"THAT YOU, LEGS?" Lucy called out, not really needing confirmation.

"Depends who's doing da asking!" shouted Legs Diamonté, peeking over the ship's rail. "IT'S ZAG AND MY KITTIES!" she yelled, gathering up her shimmery emerald-green cocktail dress in one paw. "Let's see yuh all!" she screamed excitedly, clattering towards the gangway in her high-heels then standing like film starlet at the top waving them aboard. "Come on, 'urry up," she grinned broadly, "we could do wive some customers."

Zag picked up the angrily discarded signboard then followed the twins on board.

The main deck was surprisingly tidy. The tables were partially laid and each had a parasol that fluttered in the soft breeze. A "Welcome" banner hung twisted across the poop-deck's rails with its end spilling aimlessly into the soft breeze.

Leg's sleek white fur tickled the twins' faces as she greeted them with smoochy kisses.

"Beautiful as ever," smiled Zag, "with a dress to match your eyes," he said cheekily.

"Flittery get's ya everywhere," she giggled, "not like dat jerk Catpone."

"He's still trying to woo you then?" Zag smiled.

"I'm going to wooing 'im when I get my paws on him! Ave yuh read duh garbage on dat stupid sign you're lugging?" Legs edged into a tirade.

"Um... no, as it happens," replied Zag.

"Dis is supposed t'be a classy joint an' wuh supposed t'be welcoming you all proper an' dandy like, an' dat git insists he can spill."

Zag and the twins took a closer look at the piece of ply-wood.

La MOLSEa DIck
UH ... HAY !! stop Der looking
AN seA whuts Cookin

LiT ouR GUTS giv yuh guTS a wEal going over COme SLURP A LURP CoS dey'll maKe yuh lurP

"It is a restaurant," grinned Lucy. "Flewy and Awoo are so looking forward to..."

"Yeah my kitties, and we hold finctions on board as well," Legs said excitedly. "Like wuh doing with yuh award finction. Yours is der first."

Zag wasn't quite sure how to respond, the sign certainly didn't look inviting. "The spelling?" he uttered, carefully trying hard not to offend.

"I wuz telling dat dopey block of wood Catpone dat he can't spill," said Legs scornfully. "He chucked it overboard an' went off in a puff!"

"Huff," Lucy giggled.

"Dat's what I said." Legs rummaged in her diamanté-studded shoulder bag then for a moment engaged her mouth in a top-up application of a bright-red lipstick. Even

Zag wondered if such a dainty bag was thingummagadgetal to hold the large number of cosmetics she'd crammed inside it.

"What's a lurp?" asked William, trying to work out the slogan on the sign. He was about to regret asking.

"Now dat's anuvver fing..." Legs' mouth ran into overdrive as she powdered her nose. "Guts is mad on netting 'em 'owibble slimy fings outta der sea, AN' not only dat..." she kept dabbing furiously with her powder puff, "...dey've got cweepy tentickles AN' yuh can see duh innards AN' he 'angs 'em on 'is belt tuh ripen them in der sun AN' it's disgusting AN' he's 'ad so many dere can't be many left in der sea AN' I bet he'll 'ave tuh go back to eating dose wats..."

A sudden outburst of excited yells and pandemonium emanated from the direction of the galleon's stern.

"...AN' dat's anuvver fing, dere's never a moment's peace!" she complained, clattering her heels across the main deck. "WILL YUH SHURRUP! WE'VE GOT VISITORS!"

she shouted, climbing the ladderway to the poop-deck with the bemused Zag and twins following close behind.

Trilby hat squeezed over pointy white ears, Spooky, the ship's bosun, stood prominently in the mayhem. All of the Mogster-pirate crew, a motley bunch of booted panther-like cats of varying sizes and girths, had crowded around the starboard side. Most bore scars from past fights and all looked as if the only thing that would scare them was a bar of soap. Some hung on the rigging like monkeys prancing in a tree, the rest were on deck shouting and screaming like fervent supporters watching their team in a cup-final. Frenzied splashing sounds could be heard above the noise as the crew stepped aside for Legs, Zag and the twins.

Gutrumble's ample rump protruded as he bent, struggling, over the side of the ship. He suddenly lost his balance as one of his swash-buckle-booted legs lifted off the deck. As fast as lightning, Spooky grabbed that leg and members of the crew dived at the other. Zag,

Lucy and William rushed forward and grasped Gutrumble's feet, stopping the huge cat from disappearing completely overboard. Immersed in the frenzied maul, they didn't have a clue what was happening.

"Belt it one, yuh big lummox!" yelled Legs, leaning over the side, "an' pull dat net in!"

"Whattya fink I'm twying t'do?" puffed Gutrumble, one paw wrestling a half-entangled, pug-faced creature with a tentacle coming out of its forehead, intent on bashing him with a knobbly club shaped like a giant carrot.

"What's dat it's whacking yuh wiv?" shouted Legs.

"OUCH! I'm not... OUCH! ...bovvering to... OUCH... ask!" answered Gutrumble, busily fighting to grab the club.

"Look out Guts, dere's anuver one!" exclaimed Legs, as another creature slither-sprang onto the net.

Before Gutrumble could lash out with his claw, the net broke under the strain. Both creatures fell into the sea with a huge splash, leaving Gutrumble clutching the club. "Dey've nicked my gwub!" he bawled, watching his frenzied foe vanish into a swirling vortex of water.

"Does he always fish like this?" Zag chuckled, helping to yank Gutrumble back onto the deck. "What do you do, knock them unconscious?"

"HEYYYA... ZAG!" shouted Gutrumble, waving the club in delight and doing a not-so-rapper-like jig. "Howsya doing?" Tiny black wriggly things dropped from his sleeve onto the deck as he greeted them all. "Gweat to see yuh, 'ave a memento," he grinned, handing the club to the twins.

William took it instinctively, felt it was yucky and wished he hadn't. He went to pass it to Lucy but she was preoccupied with looking sick at the sight of the slimy, limp creatures dangling around Gutrumble's belt. Trying not to attract too much attention, William quietly placed the club on a pile of old canvas sails close by.

"Uh... dat's uh... keepsick," said Catpone, arriving in a better mood.

"Keepsake, Boss," corrected Gutrumble.

"Uh... whatever," muttered Catpone, using the edge of his heel to tread a larger black wriggly thing's tail into the deck and twisting his boot to squeeze out the gooey innards like snotty toothpaste from a tube.

"Uggh dat's SOOOOH disgusting!" heaved Legs, "Wher've dose 'owwible fings come fwom?"

"I dunno, nevva seen 'em befaw," said Spooky, flicking his trilby back to low-slung, more interested in other matters. "So where's duh burdies?"

"I'm here!" said Awoo, having landed unnoticed during the commotion, "And Superdull's up there!"

"Will somebody get me down?" shrieked Flewy, tangled in the rigging for what seemed to him like an age. Spooky nipped up the rigging and quickly released Flewy to land on the lantern at the stern of the poop-deck. "I won! I won!" he squawked at Awoo, having reached the end of the *Mobsea Dick* first.

"Hey... uh, Chewy," said Catpone, adjusting his eye-patch to get a close fix on the seagull's attire.

"Dat's Flewy, Boss." Gutrumble tore off a slimy Lurklout from a bunch hanging around his waist and sucked at a tentacle. "Dis is chewy," he said, as a series of thunderous rattle-pops ripped through the air.

"PHWARR!" spluttered Spooky, unwittingly standing in the wrong place at the right time. "Stop guzzling dem 'Lurps' an' go back tuh eating dem rats cos dere far less smelly!"

"Uh... yeah... uh Screwy... uh dis ain't a fancy-dwess farty," said Catpone, trying to diplomatically change the subject in front of his guests.

"HEY! Der burdy's made'n effut!" Legs tugged Catpone's soiled tie then cuffed his ear. "Unlike you, yuh scwuffy git!"

Catpone squashed yet another black wriggly thing then drooled at Legs with his good eye. "Uh… an' tuh fink wuh not evun uh… hutched."

"Hitched, Boss," corrected Gutrumble. "Makes yuh sound like a pair of wabbits."

"Yeah… an' we could 'ave lottsa bunnies," Catpone sighed dreamily.

"Gimmee stwength!" Legs gave him a look to sink a continent. "In yuh dweams, yuh wimp! Hey Spooky, organise da party."

"Yuh heard da lady!" Spooky shouted at the crew. "An' get wid of da wigglies!"

"Hey… uh, Spooky, uh… I give da…" Already left alone to finish his sentence, Catpone wandered off to reorganise his brain, "…orders," he mumbled.

"What can we do to help?" Zag asked Legs, still chuckling at the Mogsters' banter.

"Nuffink," she smiled, "you're our guests."

"In that case we'll fetch our bags from the Beamsurfer."

"And I'll take in the view." Awoo took off, having already decided the crow's nest was a good, out-of-the-way place to doze.

"And in case you're asking," squawked

Flewy, "I'll help my friend Legs, in a super-visory capacity."

"Don't exhaust yourself," quipped Lucy.

"He loves work," Zag laughed, "he can watch others do it for days."

"Waark!" squawked Flewy, flapping his webbed foot irately. "Come on Legs, now where would you like me to perch?"

"Don't forget the keepsake, William," said Zag.

Zag and the twins chuckled away as they made their way back to the Beamsurfer. It was already great fun and they laughed about the Mogsters as they walked back along the creaking timbered wharf.

William felt his hand go slimy. "Your turn to carry this," he said, stifling a giggle as he handed the knobbly club to Lucy.

"YUK!" she yelled, "you horror, you knew it was slimy at one end."

"Hand it to me," Zag smiled, delving inside his Thingummajacket for some Eversorbent Tissues he'd invented for con-stant runny noses, "and take one of these. He wiped the club but the tissue became sopping wet and gave off a putrid rotting smell. "Darn it," he frowned, "I need to modify the absorbency ratio on these."

"Phwarr!" William screwed up his face. "And add deodoriser."

The smell went as quickly as it had come and the knobbly club shuddered in Zag's hand. "I'll register you both on the Cosmoputa." He opened the Beamsurfer's door. "Then we'll see what it knows about this."

The Putrisphere

Arm and leg contortions formed random, rubbery moulded protrusions as Eraser went bonkers, jumping around inside his Globolloon.

"STOP JUMBLING ABOUT!" Gudorphal slobber-yelled, "We're trying to have a blabber of most importance."

Eraser caught hazy glimpses of the three Lurks below each time his Globolloon briefly went transparent under the stress of his bouncing antics. Crouching down, he attempted to see more clearly by cupping his spindly hands around his eyes and pressing hard to stretch the rubbery membrane. His misty view was all the more odd for seeing a fourth Lurk who appeared to be draped in a fishing-net. Eraser watched, listening intently to the goings-on below.

"YOOOOZE LOST IT?" Gudorphal slobber-spat.

Exasperated, Malodour explained once more. "Mucid was muddled in a net frantic dabbling with a huge, black, furry cat-pirate with gut-ribbling claws and fear-trembling gnashers, dangling over the side of a silver galleon..."

"Sounds incrediblous," Putridia slurped.

"AND?" Gudorphal spittled.

"...he's pumbelting the cat-pirate with it, the cat-pirate grabbles it, I jumbles onto the net, it breaks, we fall in the sea, then I captured Mucid."

"The cat-pirate's got..." Gudorphal splurt-ed, "...GOT MY FESTALPOD?"

High above them, Eraser's ears pricked up like a coyote but he was so surprised he thought he may have misheard.

"What could I do in oodles of sunshine!" Malodour spluttered, "AND the cat-pirate had oozles of rotting Lurklouts wobbling around his waist!"

"They is being gobbled up!" splurted

Putridia. "So that's why we is losing so many!"

"THEY'S GOING TO BE GLOBOL-LISED!" Gudorphal's three tentacles angrily flexed in and out of his grisly body. "ALL OF THEM!"

Malodour's right," Putridia dribbled. "If we does that, it must covered of darkness when our powers is at the utmost tremendous."

"NO IFS! WE IS!" Gudorphal angrily grabbed his slitherstick, and wobbled furiously. "YOOZE WANTING PUTRICITY SO YOOZE NOW IS GETTING PIRATES PLENTY SHORTLY!" The flared, trumpet-like end of the stick glowed with a snotty, luminous-green bubble. "WE'LL SUCK THEIR GALLEON INTO LURKAMUNGOO!" he splurted, despatching Mucid, who remained silent, offering no resistance as it encapsulated him. "WE'LL COLONISE THEIR WORLD INTO THE GALAXY OF INCOGNITO!"

Eraser watched the horrid Globolloon

drift upwards towards him, its luminosity casting even more macabre shadows across the dank cavern. Joining the sinister cluster in the conical roof, it settled alongside Eraser, bumping his protruding, cling-wrapped nose in the process.

"Yooze ready ourselfs!" Gudorphal commanded. "Putridia, preparate the Putrisphere. Malodour, you is making sure every slitherstick's full loaded with putricity currents. I'll go and assembles together the Lurkwarriors."

"I HOPE THEY CLAW YOUR GUTS OUT!" Eraser shouted at them. "AND YOU!" he yelled, redirecting his wrath at Mucid's Globolloon next to him. "STOP FIDGETING AND SAY SOMETHING HELPFUL!"

"Not much to blabber about," Mucid spluttered.

"Not surprised considering you didn't even try to fight your way out of this mess!" Eraser scoffed.

"Don't need to!" Mucid busied himself,

nudging Eraser's Globolloon in the process.

"WILL YOU STOP NUDG... What d'you mean you don't need to?"

"I've got Festalmaggots."

"That's all I need!" Eraser shuddered, thinking what with Globscurity looming and now Festalmaggots, luck was not on his side. "Is that a terminal disease or what?"

"No, they is what I did tooken from the Festalpod."

Eraser smirked, realising he had heard Gudorphal correctly. He knew of the Festalpod's powers from a long time ago. He'd even tried to steal it but it went missing before he could. Somehow he had to escape and that had seemed impossible until now. "You can get out of here?"

"They grows into Lurklouts and then into Lurkwarriors, and they is my meanings of escape."

"It could take ages for them to do that, you Boghead!"

"I only needs uses while they're maggots, stupid!"

"DON'T CALL ME STU..."

"You is mouth-blabbering too loudly!" splurted Mucid. "Their acidspittle breaks down the Globolloon skins then they gobble them and anything all, if it stays still enough."

"What about me?"

"Don't stay still," slurped Mucid, still nudging Eraser's Globolloon.

"I MEANT, CAN..." Eraser, did his level best to sound friendly whilst having to converse with what he already classed an idiot, "...can you get me out as well?"

"Why should I?" asked Mucid.

"Because," Eraser began to fume, "I know all about the Mogsters, that's why!"

"Mogsters?"

"The gangster cat-pirates who've nicked the Festalpod off you!"

"Interesting," slurped Mucid, still bumping around. "I'll see!"

"What d'you mean you'll..." Eraser suddenly felt some heavy tugging at the top of the cluster of Globolloons. "There's no time to see!"

"You is saying yooze agree to help me get the Festalpod?"

"YES!"

"Strict timing is called for," said Mucid. "Yooze to ask questions no more and not mouth-blabber. The Lurkwarriors will tow our cluster to the adjoining cavern of the Putrisphere, but just before we's fed in our Globolloons will be dropped to the ground. At that precise moment I release the Festalmaggots, they munch a hole in our Globolloons and yooze to follow me. Got that?"

"Got it," Eraser replied, falling backwards as the cluster was jerked and dragged around like a bunch of party balloons. Just as they were towed inside the Putrisphere's cavern, the pressure of Mucid's Globolloon began to subside and a dark, nibbling patch appeared on the outside of Eraser's Globolloon. Cringing at the sight of black, pulsating Festalmaggots vomiting acidspittle and chewing like fury, he escaped through the hole made in his membraned prison. Under the cover of the cluster, Eraser crawled soggily across the slimy cavern and followed Mucid to hide in a thin crevice.

Goo-pumping walls splurted with bursts of obnoxious gas. The whole place looked worse than the inside of a gigantic stomach suffering with gastric problems. At the centre of this gurgling expanse wobbled the Putrisphere, the size of a hot-air balloon. Yellowish-white in colour, it throbbed with a network of glowing red veins, like a gigantic pulsating eyeball infected with severe conjunctivitis. Thick stretchy ligaments of brownish-green sinew, tacky with slime, adhered the steaming monstrosity to the cavern floor. At its base, a horrid gaping vent with the appearance of a gulleted fish's undercarriage heaved and foamed ooze-bubbling goo.

Mucid and Eraser remained deathly still as they watched a long, putrid chain of Lurkwarriors, linked by their tentacles, sucker-heave the cluster of writhing

Globolloons into the Putrisphere's hot flapping vent. Even the most faded made a last desperate pounding attempt to escape from their globular prisons. With a slurp louder than ten thousand emptying plug-holes, the victims were sucked inside as easily as jelly off a plate, drained of all their energy and vaporised into Globscurity, to be lost forever.

In no time at all a load of putricity currents, each one the size of an egg, rolled down a chute into rubbery sacks held open by a gang of Lurkwarriors. Putridia picked some out at random to inspect their quality and check the glimmer-value. With one on each sucker-ended finger, she held her three tentacular arms in the air and they shone like neon bulbs on a grotesque set of candelabras. "S'not bad!" she slobber-cackled loudly. "And there is being lots lots more soon."

Eraser noticed another group of Lurkwarriors struggling with a bunch of snaking pipes growing out of the side of the Putrisphere. A thick, dark yellow paste suddenly spurted forth then, as it flowed smoothly, they directed each pipe into long tubes with bulbous ends. "What's going on over there?" he asked Mucid.

"Puspirating," replied Mucid. "They is making slithersticks from the Putrisphere's sweat glands."

"That really is nasty," Eraser gagged. "Now let's get out of here!"

Cosmoputing

Meanwhile, the twins were sitting next to Zag inside the Beamsurfer, looking into the spherical network of purpled light that formed the Cosmoputa's vista-globe. Completely absorbed in what they were doing, none of them noticed the sporadic shudders of the knobbly club lying on the floor of the Beamsurfer.

Zag took out one of the items Lucy had put in his seat compartment before they left his barn.

"Now let's see what happens," he said expectantly, pointing the Astromistical Spray-Capsule into the vista-globe.

No sooner had he pressed the small nozzle, than a host of astromistic particles darted around inside the vista-globe, like excited tiny firebirds coming home to roost. For a moment, Lucy and William were awe-struck as the particles formed a golden elongated figure of eight which slowly twirled in its splendorous orbit.

"That's Astral's symbol, the sign of infinity. You must keep quiet whatever happens," whispered Zag, sensing the twins about to jump up and down in excitement.

"Please remain still while your molecular structure is scanned and your genetic code established," said the Cosmoputa.

The golden sign of infinity twirled faster and faster and faster until it became a blur. Then suddenly from out of the vista-globe a swirling cosmic cloak of mist enveloped the twins, fizzing every colour of the rainbow.

"Hello, Lucy and William," said the Cosmoputa, as the cosmic cloak of fiery colours subsided into the tinted purple hue of the vista-globe. "Welcome to the Infinet."

"I've created both your genetic access recognition profiles," Zag grinned, completing the twins registration. "Now you can log on without me."

Lucy giggled impishly. "Just think how

it'll help with our homework."

"Oh great!" William grunted. "That's the last thing I want to think of!"

"Come on," Zag smiled, "how about us doing some homework on that knobbly club?"

"Peripheral Systems Reminder!" The Cosmoputa displayed a floating icon. "Do you wish to activate the Cosmo-fobs?"

"Glad you mentioned that," said Zag, taking out the three remaining items from his seat compartment. Lucy and William looked curiously at each other, wondering what was coming next. "These Cosmo-fobs are proto-types," Zag started to explain, handing them one each, "and are rather like…"

"A key-fob torch," interrupted William examining it, "but without a key ring."

"More like a highly polished pebble." Lucy inspected hers closely and found a tiny crystal-like bulb, inset into the flat of the oval shape.

"They're pocket-size Cosmoputas." Zag chuckled, pointing at the 'activate' icon floating in the vista-globe, "but smaller by far and much more advanced than any palm-held computer."

"Can I try it?" asked William enthusiastically.

"Ladies first," Zag grinned, showing Lucy how to hold the Cosmo-fob by keeping the crystal upwards in the palm of her hand. "They respond to your thoughts. You think it open."

"Think it open?" Lucy looked puzzled.

"Mind activation," Zag smiled. "It's as simple as making a wish."

"Don't just stare at it, you must wish it to start up," William said impatiently to Lucy.

"Will you shush!" Lucy scolded, shutting her eyes to concentrate. Like a fountain of stardust, a vista-globe burst out of her Cosmo-fob.

"Can I have a go now?" asked William, aching for his turn and holding his Cosmo-fob the correct way up in his palm.

"Let me explain," Zag smiled patiently. "With these Cosmo-fobs we can keep in spoken and visual contact with each other whenever needed. But remember at this stage we're really just testing them."

"What shall I do next, then?" asked Lucy, thrilled with the whole idea.

"Think about being warm," said Zag.

Lucy concentrated and was instantly wrapped in a colourful haze, her whole being taking on a glow. William was so intrigued he forgot his impatience and waited for Lucy to say something. She didn't utter a word.

"Come on," said Zag, eager to know all was well, "tell us how it feels."

"Lovely and cosy," Lucy sighed contentedly. "Very cosy in fact."

"Fantastic!" Zag proudly stroked his beard. "I've also programmed in other thingummagadgetal qualities. That particular one I developed from the bragbag full of hot air."

"Brrr, I'm freezing!" Lucy shivered.

Zag's face dropped as she took on a bluish glow. "Don't say it's playing up already!" he implored, raising his hands in frustration.

"Just testing," she giggled, returning to normal, "I tried cold, that's all."

"Cheeky," Zag laughed, as Lucy put the Cosmo-fob away in her jeans pocket.

"Don't fool about, Lucy, this is serious stuff!" complained William, still itching to test his own.

Zag savoured the urgent look of expectancy on William's face. "Okay, now it's your turn."

"Watch this space!" shouted William, full of confidence. Mind-activating his Cosmo-fob, it burst out in a brilliance of colour. "Whey hey!" he shouted, gleefully. "And for my next trick I'll..."

"Don't do anything silly!" Lucy bossed, apprehensive about her brother's showing off.

"Try the Chameleoniser function," Zag quickly suggested. "Just wish to hide yourself."

William blended into the background of the Beamsurfer's interior. "Good eh?" said William, very pleased with himself. "BOO!"

It was only when he moved that the background rippled with distortion.

"You must keep still," Zag instructed, "like a real Chameleon. Do that and it will be virtually impossible for anyone to see you."

"IT MOVED!" Lucy yelled in alarm, as something touched her foot.

"It's only Gutrumble's knobbly club," scoffed William, shutting down his Cosmofob, "you are a scaredy-cat."

"I'm not!" said Lucy giving William an icy stare.

"No need for that," said Zag, firmly. He picked up the knobbly club and it gave him a jolt as if trying to escape out of his hand.

"See, it did move!" said Lucy. "It only frightened me for a second 'cos it was unexpected."

"Enough to make anybody jump," said Zag, presenting the knobbly club into the Cosmoputa's vista-globe. "Now let's see what we can find out about this."

"Didn't make me jump," said William, cockily.

"The item is now scanned," said the Cosmoputa. "Please remove and wait for the analysis."

Zag took a Thingummagadgetal Self-sizing Carrier Bag out of his Thingummajacket and, as he looked at the messy floor, he wished he'd thought of that beforehand. Invented for Christmas supermarket shopping, the bag adjusted its size as Zag put the slimy club inside it. Placing the bag by his feet, he sat with the twins, gazing into the tinted hue of the vista-globe and patiently waited for the result of the scan.

"Waaark!" screeched Flewy, making William jump as he landed unexpectedly just inside the Beamsurfer's open door. "That ship's full of wrigglies!"

"Please wait," the Cosmoputa requested.

"Don't we all look ever so busy!" mocked Flewy, scratching himself.

Zag kept his eyes fixed on the Cosmoputa. "Seeing as you're Supergull, we thought you'd be busy helping Legs."

"Please wait," the Cosmoputa requested

once again.

"If you're watching telly, I'd try a different channel!" Flewy quipped.

"This one's okay, thank you," giggled Lucy. "It's about seagulls with a sense of humour."

"Please wait," the Cosmoputa requested.

"Trouble is they can't find any," laughed William.

"Very funny," squawked Flewy, not amused.

"We're waiting for the analysis of this club," Zag sighed, gazing at the twirling sign of infinity. "Even I didn't think it would take this long."

"Please wait," the Cosmoputa requested again.

"Huh! I get better customer service from my utilities company," Flewy remarked, "and that's saying something!"

"You don't have utilities," said Zag.

"You've missed my point!" Flewy huffed, "I meant…"

"Please wait," the Cosmoputa instructed,

"you are being referred."

"SEE what I mean!" squawked Flewy, perching on the back of Zag's seat. "They'll be playing silly music next!"

"Hey COOOOL!" shouted William, hugging Lucy in excitement. "Look at that!" The sign of infinity dissolved into a floating Orb of Brilliance. The gleaming symbol of the Galaxy of Ideas signalled something special was about to happen.

"Don't say they've lost that again!" beaked Flewy. "That's what started it all off last time!"

"You are not alone," said the Cosmoputa.

"That is COOOOL!" Flewy scoffed. "Anyone could work that out!"

"To proceed further your guest must either leave or be registered," the Cosmoputa instructed.

"Flewy, wait outside for a moment please," said Zag, conscious of the evening sun, the Mogsters, and not wishing to delay the analysis further.

"ME!" Flewy squawked, insulted, overcome with curiosity and not making a move. "Wait outside! If that's ASTRAL, ask him about my AWARD."

"It's just a technicality, so for the moment please do as I ask," said Zag firmly. "Just let me see what's going on."

"So now I'm just a technicality!" Flewy screeched. "I know when I'm not wanted!" He flapped out of the Beamsurfer and plonked himself next to the craft. "Why I came here in the first place I don't know," he ranted to himself. The cockpit door closed, leaving him to stand, beak aloft, wings on hips, and work out a way of nose-beaking into what was happening. "And anyway this place is full of bugs too!" he squawked, flicking a black wriggly thing with his foot. "Bet this wouldn't have happened to Awoo!" he muttered, slapping the ground repeatedly with his foot then flicking another wriggly.

Zag settled back into his seat. "It's just Lucy, William and I here now," he said, concentrating on the Cosmoputa.

The screen glowed a spectrum of colours

and the floating silver orb delicately splayed open like flowering petals on a spring day. "Welcome to the Galactic Circle Conference Room."

Suddenly, Astral's face appeared in the centre of the sparkling hue. His curling blond locks of hair accentuated his chiselled features and his deep blue eyes gleamed generously. "Hello my friends," he greeted. "Where are you?"

"Hi, what a surprise!" said Zag, "We're on the Island of Radiance, didn't you know?"

"Oh dear," said Astral apologetically, "I had asked the Mogsters to inform me of your arrival."

"Well we're here," Zag chuckled, a little embarrassed at inadvertently imposing himself on Astral.

"Your Cosmoputa is working well," Astral congratulated. "It searched the Infinet, recognised you as a Fellow of the Galactic Circle and gave you access to me."

· "It's just that I thought this thing odd enough to test my Cosmoputa," said Zag, "but I didn't mean to trouble you with it."

"You're always more than welcome." Astral's handsome face radiated a warm smile. "In fact you've made a crucial discovery. You have somehow found the Festalpod."

"What's a Festalpod?" Zag asked Astral, ignoring the sudden knocking on the outside of the Beamsurfer.

"It's a vital part of the Juvitree, unique to Telijencia, the Island of Forgotten Ideas," replied Astral. "The Festalpod has to remain inside the Juvitree to control the lush, delicate beauty and inspirational ecology of the island."

"We'll take it back for you," said Lucy, obligingly. "Won't we Zag?"

"Just tell us how to get there and we'll do it right away," Zag nodded in agreement. "Flewy's outside, so he can tell the Mogsters to delay the party."

"I wish it were that easy," replied Astral. "It's very strange, it was lost with Telijencia when the whole island itself vanished from the World of Creativity many years ago."

"Did anybody inhabit the island?" Zag asked.

"A nice Rutilan man and wife who caretakered the island for us, but they were lost as well," said Astral, with sadness. "I dread to think how they must have suffered."

"Telijencia sounds like Atlantis," remarked Lucy. "They must have drowned."

"Yeah, that sank in the ocean," William added, helpfully. "Have you looked there?"

"We've searched for it everywhere for years, without success," said Astral. "Throughout the Galaxies. We think Eraser wanted to get his evil hands on it to steal the forgotten ideas and make them all bad. He actually helped search for Telijencia before he turned traitor and tried to rule the World of Creativity and Galaxy of Ideas by stealing the Orb of Brilliance."

"Well we stopped him doing that," said Zag, "so at least the Festalpod's in safe hands and Eraser's rotting in the depths of the ocean."

"The real problem now is that the Festalpod is not only vital to Telijencia's survival but also to recycling good ideas for the future of all creativity." Astral looked very concerned. "It the only way the bad forgotten ideas can be cleansed into good ideas."

Zag lifted his fez and scratched his head. "So what's been happening to Telijencia without the Festalpod, I wonder?"

"I dread to think." Astral looked severely worried. "If the island's been left to go wild, slowly but surely every galaxy throughout the universe will totally succumb to the influence of bad ideas."

"But if you can't find the island, how do you know it still exists?" Lucy asked Astral.

"Good question, Lucy." Astral smiled at her perceptiveness. "The Festalpod will only exist while Telijencia exists. Therefore its very existence is proof."

"Then somehow we must find Telijencia and restore the balance," said Zag, rubbing his beard. "It could of course also mean that for some reason, something or someone has been meddling with that island ever since you lost it." Zag looked very thoughtful. "Even more interesting because it was long before Eraser turned bad."

"Which is why I need a favour from Lucy and William," Astral smiled. "I'm hoping you'll let me borrow Zag for a short while. I promise we'll have the party as soon as possible."

"But Lucy and I want to help you," said William, disappointedly.

"We won't get in your way," added Lucy.

"I know you won't," smiled Astral, finding it difficult to convince the twins, "but I need to talk with Zag first of all, as soon as I can."

"We can carry on talking as we are now," William quickly added, as even more noise could be heard from outside the Beamsurfer.

"Listen, you two tinkers," said Zag softly, "it could be very dangerous and I need to find out some more about all this first. You know you can always come with me when it's at all possible."

"What if I send Eggbert and Eggna to see you while Zag and I talk?" Astral suggested.

These two huge powerful eagles soared the Galaxy of Ideas as Elan the Spirit of Vigour – he balanced power and strength, and Vertu the Spirit of Style – she turned the special into extra special. This was great incentive indeed, a rare privilege and one the twins didn't expect. Lucy and William knew the eagles as plain Eggbert and Eggna, both of whom had become their close friends during the time of 'Blot' and the treacherous rule of Eraser. In fact it was Eggbert who had saved Lucy from drowning during the times of such evil. Even so, the twins were determined to negotiate not missing out on any possible adventure.

"And you and Zag promise to let us help you, after your chat?" said Lucy.

"And you'll let us know what you ask Zag to do before he does it?" said William, adding to what had become a verbal contract.

"It's a deal," replied Astral.

The twins sought each others approval and whispered to one another. Neither of them was happy but felt under the circumstances this was the best they could negotiate. They gave their official verdict.

"It's a deal," said Lucy, reluctantly.

"Yep, that's the deal," agreed William, wondering what else he could have negotiated.

"That's all agreed then," said Zag; he too wanted to get the meeting over with quickly and return to the twins. "Trouble is we'll get no peace to talk if you come here," said Zag, as the banging on the Beamsurfer showed no sign of letting up, "nor on the *Mobsea Dick* for that matter."

"We'll meet on the Cameracraft-carrier section of the *Sea Err*," suggested Astral. "It's easy for you to land the Beamsurfer on the carrier deck, and it's still separated from the *Sea Err* itself. With no Eraser to bother us any more it's deserted and peaceful."

"Good, I won't be too far away," Zag

winked at the twins, "only just around the coast from here."

"Lucy and William can help keep the Mogsters happy," suggested Astral. "We don't want them to think they're being ignored."

"I still wish we could come," said Lucy, "but promise not to keep Zag too long."

"I promise," Astral smiled.

"Let's hope the Festalpod will lead us to Telijencia." Zag was more than delighted to squeeze in some detective work during their visit.

"We need to know how it got here," said Astral.

"That's easy," William replied, "Gutrumble gave it to us as a keepsake."

"He was fishing at the time, so Telijencia might have sunk into the sea after all," Lucy chipped in, still progressing her own Atlantis theory.

The thumping on the door became more urgent, accompanied by squawking and shouting. "Sounds like the party's already started," Astral laughed. "No problem, we'll have two." He waved. "Zag, we'll meet just after sunset." Astral's image faded into the ether.

"WE'RE COMING!" Zag chuckled, shutting down the Cosmoputa. He slid open the door, with the twins following, and stopped in amazement. "Hey Legs! How often does this happen?"

"First time ever!" she said. She was wearing a pair of Catpone's boots and squelching wrigglies like fury. "Wuh infested wid duh blighters an' we really gotta make sail quick!" she urged.

"I could've been eaten!" Flewy shrieked, fully goggled, hovering wildly above a multiplying mass of squirming blackness. Like hot tarmac it spread across the ground and some slithered up the Beamsurfer.

"Wuh gotta go!" Legs flustered, flicking some wrigglies off her slinky-slit party dress. "Wuh'll be well wid of dem wigglies out at sea!"

Lucy and William grimaced as Zag

carefully picked one off between thumb and
forefinger, avoiding the small but munching
jaws filled with tiny, ravenous, piranha-like
teeth. It visibly grew as if fit to burst. "Lucy,
William, you go with Legs." Zag crunched
the wriggly with his boot. "And Flewy can
help me..."

"To make sure everybody gets to the ship
safely," Flewy interrupted, flying off in a
hurry.

Just a Whiffing Waft!

Mucid slither-led the way into a tubelike alleyway and through a putrid, slime-curtained maze. The surface slopped heavily beneath Eraser's sodden pirate boots as step by step he sank ankle-deep into the gunge.

"Now where are we going?" he panted.

"To get some slithersticks and get out of here," slobber-whispered Mucid, pointing to a gunge-flapping opening. "Stay here, don't make a babble, I'll be back soon."

Glad of the rest, Eraser watched Mucid slither out of sight. His pirate finery was ruined – the orange shirt-ruffles drooped, the purple tailed-coat hung limp. He swore silent revenge on Zag, Astral, the twins, the Mogste... His evil compilation was disrupted by the sound of Putridia and Gudorphal's angry voices on the other side of membraned wall.

"BUT it's the FESTALPOD'S spawning

season!" splurted Putridia.

"AND I SAYS that's to our advantage!" Gudorphal slobber-shouted.

"And I SAYS it'll need REPLENISH-ING!" slurped Putridia.

"THEN I SAYS we take it to the JUVIT-REE!" blasted Gudorphal.

"J...Juvitree!" Eraser muffled a splutter of disbelief and listened harder.

Putridia kept pestering in full flow. "SO! What if we can't get the FESTALPOD off them?"

"SIMPLE," yell-splattered Gudorphal, fed up with her interfering. "We use the Lurkwarriors to make a vortex around their ship, suck them into the Lake of Lost Ideas, globollize them, THEN you can putrify the cat-pirates at your leisure!"

"THEN why didn't you say so?" Putridia slobber-spat.

"BECAUSE YOOZE WON'T SHUT UP!"

"No need to keep splurting," Putridia spittled.

"YOOZE concentrate on all the putricity we'll capture, and LEAVE THE REST TO ME!"

"They've found Telijencia!" A sickly grin spewed thin across Eraser's pallid face as the quarrelsome Lurks faded from earshot. "It's got to be somewhere in the Galaxy of Incognito," he figured, "and Mucid must know of its whereabouts." Revenge raced through his mind: deposing the Master of the Galaxy of Ideas, regaining the Orb of Brilliance containing the four interlocking stones of Skill: Blue, Inspiration, Imagination and Genius. He smirked gleefully. "I'll capture the ideas of Telijencia and starve the World of Creativity!" He was so ecstatic, he shook from head to toe, only the tacky slime on his boots restraining him from hopping with delight.

Mucid returned with two slithersticks. "No use yooze looking impatient, that was very trickley," he slurped, handing one to Eraser. "Malodour was checking the Lurkwarriors were fully loading their slithersticks with putricity currents."

"So what do I do with this, wave it like a magic wand?"

"Simple, yooze fly on it."

"And how am I supposed to do that?"

"Like a witch on a broomstick. It'll go slippy-glidey-whoosh and faster than lightning."

"Are you telling me I've got to sit on this thing?"

"Or yooze stay here and is globollised," Mucid splurted nonchalantly. "I was thinking," said Eraser, putting on a friendly tone of voice, "we're in Lurkamungoo, in the Cesslesstial Galaxy of Incognito, is that right?"

Mucid briefly explained. "You is somewhere and nowhere..."

It would take a little time for Eraser to comprehend that this galaxy was the ultimate place of nothingness – so unreal it was real – a desert in the Universe of Imagination – a black hole of nightmares far from everywhere and everyone yet very close to anywhere and anybody. But if he did know that if he discovered the secret of getting and out of this Galaxy, he would find Telijencia.

"...so's you is everywhere you'll never know, the last place yooze would never think of!" dribbled Mucid.

"So where exactly is the Galaxy of Incognito?" asked Eraser.

"That's a secret, otherwise it wouldn't be Incognito now, would it?"

"Is Incognito made up of lost places?"

"You is asking questions too many!" splurted Mucid. Having discovered Mucid's measure, Eraser smirked to himself and pretended to be apologetic. "Quite right, neither the time nor the place," he said, about to straddle the slitherstick.

Mucid swiftly sucker-grabbed Eraser. "Wait for the vibrations! We must wait till they leave."

"What vibra..." A tremendous whooosh shook Eraser and the whole cavernous web of membrane, "...tionssssss?"

"That's the Lurkwarriors leaving," spluttered Mucid. "With that lot Gudorphal really means business."

"So do I!" Eraser's face puked a smirk. "How long will it take to get back to my island?"

"One waft," slurped Mucid.

"What's a waft?" Eraser grunted impatiently.

"A waft's a whirlwind tunnel of whoosh that takes us to wherever-whenever within sixty whiffs," dribbled Mucid.

"Then why didn't you say so?" barked Eraser. "STOP messing me about and TAKE me to the *Sea Err*!"

"The *Sea Err*?"

"My ship!" said Eraser.

"Wait a whiffing waft!" Mucid splurted. "The Festalpod's not on your ship, it's on the silver galleon!"

"Exactly!" said Eraser, belittling Mucid's outburst. "That's why we need my ship, it's much bigger, far superior and..." He stopped short of further explanation in case Mucid got the wrong or the right idea, depending on the point of view. "...If you want the Festalpod, I need my ship and you need to stop prattling on and show me how to fly this thing!"

Getting the 'hang' of flying a slitherstick was too literal for Eraser's liking. To prevent falling off he almost made a dreadful error shoving it up his trouser-leg. "This is totally undignified!" he raved, taking more care and managing to navigate it under his trousers, under his shirt and out through his collar. "It's like being hung sideways on a coat-hang..." he yelled, squirting into the swirling waft, downside-up with arms and one spindly leg thrashing akimbo.

Within sixty whiffs they were circling the Island of Radiance. The sunset hesitated to dip a gentle toe into the calm sea as putrid blotches of darkness swept across its surface, partially blemishing the reddish-glow.

"We must be careful," warned Mucid, "there's Gudorphal and his Lurkwarriors waiting for the sun to go down."

"There she is, THERE SHE IS!" Eraser yelled excitedly, dangling by the seat of his pants and showing no concern to Mucid's warning. "I'll GET YOU BACK IN ACTION!" he shouted, determined never again to let his pride and joy look so hopeless.

In the times of 'Blot' the awesome *Sea Err* had housed his terrifying squadron of Cameracraft on its detachable flight-deck carrier. In those days it had looked like an incredible cross between a galleon and aircraft carrier. Isolated by the events of the past, the 'carrier' remained separated on the opposite side of the lagoon. Its mother ship, the *Sea Err*, lay deserted, anchored in the same spot where Eraser had made his escape from Astral and Zag before crashing into the sea.

Mucid landed stealthily on the eerie deserted galleon and Eraser belly-flopped onto the deck beside him.

"Glad that bit's over," Eraser squelched, ridding himself of his slitherstick. He peered around and about him; his ship had been left exactly as it was when he fled from it. "Lazy minds, lost opportunities," he muttered, thinking about the Mogsters. "They'll need all their remaining eight lives this time round."

"We's got t'be getting the Festalpod from the cat-pirates before Gudorphal does!" Mucid splurted, impatient at the sight of Eraser's dawdling.

A wet shadowy figure leapt from the bulwark, sending Eraser sprawling.

He freed himself and rolled over to the base of the main mast to grab a sturdy belaying-pin; normally used to secure ropes it also made a good truncheon. He couldn't believe what he was seeing as more of the shadowy raiding party jumped onto the deck. Mucid pointed his slitherstick, out of which he intended to fire a Globolloon at their attackers.

"STOP!" yelled Eraser, recognising them, "They're my Eradicators!"

"Eradicators?" splurted Mucid.

"My men! My team!" Eraser said, rather surprised but just as proud.

"It is you, isn't it?" gasped a soaking wet Eradicator, gawping at Eraser's ruined pirate finery and assisting him to his feet. "We all thought you were at the bottom of the ocean."

"OF COURSE IT'S ME, YOU IDIOT! AND I'M NOT!" Eraser bawled. "MORE TO THE POINT, WHERE HAVE YOU LOT ALL SPRUNG FROM?"

The Eradicators stood soggily to

attention, saluted Eraser and, soaking wet, explained. "After Astral defeated us..."

"I DON'T WISH TO BE REMINDED," Eraser shouted, not wanting his 'dirty washing' hung in front of Mucid. "SO GET ON WITH IT!"

"...and after you were sunk in the sea..."

"I WASN'T SUNK, I CRASHED!"

"...A...Astral forced us to remain on the Island of Radiance to help the Rutilans restore the island and rebuild their villages."

"WHAT?" Eraser blasted. "What's this RADIANCE bit? THIS IS BLOT!"

"Astral renamed the island so now it's called..."

"I KNOW WHAT YOU SAID!" Eraser fumed. "WE'LL SOON SEE ABOUT THAT!" He dismissed the Eradicators with a flick of his hand. "AND for your sakes I hope you did a BAD JOB!" Eraser added, turning to face Mucid.

"B...but Sar!" said the Eradicator nervously. "I thought I should warn you about..."

"HAVEN'T YOU GONE YET?" yelled Eraser. Suddenly, he stopped to think. "WARN ME... ABOUT WHAT?"

"The island's infested with black, wriggly things that burst and turn into horrible, slimy, sucker-legged bigger things, SAR!" The Eradicator realised he'd gained Eraser's full attention and continued. "They chew everything in sight... the Rutilans that were guarding us ran off and that's how we escaped."

"We's must hurry before Gudorphal creates a vortex," Mucid splurted impatiently.

"Then go and do something useful," Eraser barked at the Eradicator, "LIKE MAKING SURE NONE OF YOU HAVE BROUGHT ANY ON BOARD!" Eraser peered purposefully at Mucid. "What's this about a vortex?"

"An enormous whirlpool in the sea. It'll suck the cat-pirates and their galleon into..." Mucid hesitated.

"And where exactly will they be sucked into?" Eraser asked.

"Yooze s'not getting not the point!" Mucid splurted.

"THEN WHAT IS THE POINT?" Eraser shouted impatiently.

"THE POINT IS!" splurt-blasted Mucid, "IF that happens I'LL never get the Festalpod! Gudorphal GETS control over the next spawning of Festalmaggots! AND BANG GOES MY ARMY OF WAR-RIORS!"

"WELL NOW we can't let that happen, CAN WE?" Eraser smirked, realising Mucid had no clue that the real value of the spawning was the rejuvenation of forgotten ideas, not the creation of mutated maggots. "Wait here, my friend, I need to fetch something that's very important to both of us. I'll be back in a whiff."

Eraser could hardly believe his luck as he scampered to his cabin. Things had already gone well and now they were getting even better. He grinned evilly as he opened his antique desk drawer and found his flashgun. Rummaging through the contents of another drawer he pulled out a pack of 'prismatrans' which he loaded into the handle of his flash-gun. The size of a playing card and just as slender, each prismatran not only captured the holographical image but also the very being of whoever was unfortunate enough to be caught by the flash.

"Don't stand there dripping!" Eraser barked, shoving an Eradicator out of the way as he rushed back to the top deck. "READY THE SHIP!"

"Hurry up!" slurped Mucid, wobbling like an anxious jelly stranded on a bouncy castle.

"Now where's my slitherstick?" Eraser panted.

"It's by the mast!" splurted Mucid, fast losing his patience.

"Trust me," Eraser smiled, taking Mucid's slitherstick and placing it neatly next to his.

"What is yooze doing now?" asked Mucid.

"I'm going to find the FESTALPOD!" Eraser bawled, his piggy eyes nearly bulging out of their sockets, "WITHOUT YOU!" Mucid looked dumbstruck as he watched Eraser pace up and down the deck.

"We is not got time for messling about!" Mucid splurted, his forehead arm flexing nervously. "WHAT ABOUT OUR DEAL?"

"LISTEN YOU MUTANT MAGGOT!" Eraser stuck his spindly forefinger in his ear and vigorously waggled some wax. "THE DEAL'S OFF!"

"Wait a whiffing waft!" splattered Mucid, "YOOZE CAN'T DO THAT!"

"Oh yes I can!" Eraser smirked, "AND I can do THIS!" He fired his flash-gun and ejected the playing card sized prismatran from its handle. Mucid's shocked holographic image looked as if it had been frozen in a sliver of clear ice. Eraser grinned evilly at the image. "NOBODY MESSES WITH ERASER THE TERRIBLE!"

"Anything I can do, SAR?" said a freshly uniformed Eradicator.

"YOU AGAIN!" With a fixed gaze, Eraser circled around the Eradicator as if giving an inspection. "SO glad you've found time look smart," he said.

"SAR!" saluted the Eradicator. "Shall I arrange for the ship's lanterns to be lit soon?"

"NO! But as you're so keen to please," Eraser eyeballed him and stripped down to his baggy underpants, throwing each slimy item into the Eradicator's squirming face. "CHUCK THOSE CLOTHES OVER-BOARD, PREPARE THE MASTS FOR RETRACTION, THEN REPORT TO ME IN MY CABIN!" he barked. "GET YOUR PRIORITIES RIGHT AND MAKE SURE MY SHIP REMAINS IN BLACKOUT!"

The Eradicators stared as a scrawny, pimple-ridden body ran past them like an emaciated ostrich searching for its feathers. Eraser quickly chose another pirate outfit from the many identical ones hanging neatly in the wardrobe which stretched the full width of his cabin. He had hardly finished dressing when there came a knock on his cabin door.

"ENTER!" shouted Eraser, adjusting the

ruffles on his orange shirt and preening himself in his long, splendid mirror.

"Ship's prepared for conversion, SAR!" saluted the Eradicator.

Eraser sat down at his antique desk, reached for his quill pen and pulled it like a lever. The wood panelling in front of him opened, revealing a large screen. He twisted the pen and the surface of the desk parted, giving him access to a control panel. At the press of a button, each of the galleon's masts retracted like telescopes. Then the furled sails folded umbrella-like, as each section of the mast closed into itself. He pressed another button and transparent glass-like canopies, the full length of the hull, rose out of both sides of the galleon, meeting in the middle and making a water-tight cover over the entire ship. The *Sea Err* had become a submarine.

The Eradicator watched keenly as Eraser highlighted a menu on the screen and clicked on the words; *'Lock onto Mobsea Dick'*. "We'll be keeping track of you," Eraser cackled to himself. "What are you doing wandering across my CABIN?" he yelled at the Eradicator.

"Sorry, Sar!" said the Eradicator, pointing out of the large stern windows. "But there's something landing across the water on the old carrier-deck, SAR!"

Eraser picked up his brass telescope and rushed to look. "Well, well, well," he smirked, recognising the Beamsurfer, "LOOK WHAT'S JUST ARRIVED?"

"What do we do? SAR!"

"We watch, wait, remain vigilant and be ready to move immediately at my command." Eraser grinned evilly. "Because I know more than they know and KNOWLEDGE IS POWER!" With one hand, he reached for the wine decanter on the table nearby, not taking his pig-like eyes off the carrier-deck for one moment. "What's more, they think I'm history!"

"It's empty, SAR!" said the Eradicator.

"THEN FILL IT AND POUR TWO DRINKS!" Eraser ordered. "You're promoted to second-in-command designate. What's your name anyway?"

"Shystar, Sar!" he said, handing Eraser a goblet of wine.

"Sounds appropriate," said Eraser, making a toast to the *Sea Err*. "Even the high seas have trembled in her ghostly wake. She's cast fear everywhere!" he reminisced, with evil pride and between sips. "Her huge black bow emerging from her dark, misty shroud, into the moonlight... the tops of her tall masts partially hidden by the mist..." His piggy eyes stared, icily happy. "...Her enormous black sails bulging with the strain of the wind." Eraser suddenly laughed manically. "BUT there was never any wind! And by the time my prey had realised THAT it was TOOOOO late!" Eraser suddenly shoved his goblet into Shystar's hand. "FILL IT UP and then listen hard!"

Shystar did what he was asked and waited.

"This ship of mine can go anywhere, even under water. Play your cards right and you will be PRIVILEGED to see its FULL POTENTIAL!" Eraser pointed out of his cabin window. "The moment that craft takes off, we go at lightning speed to find the *Mobsea Dick* and enter the vortex whirlpool Mucid was on about, without even the Lurks knowing!"

Infestered!

Lucy and William had little time to think about Eggbert and Eggna arriving or anything else other than the task in which they were involved – it seemed never-ending. With shovel and broom they worked very hard helping the Mogsters clear the wrigglies off the *Mobsea Dick*, filling buckets full of the horrid creatures. As these were dumped overboard even more appeared. As well as nipping at the scuffling pirate boots, the wrigglies had also become very partial to munching the deck timbers.

Awoo had abandoned his doze in the crow's-nest and was also helping to search for new outbreaks of this infestation. The sun had almost set and he was busy lighting the ship's lanterns. "Somebody ought to close those," he hooted at Catpone.

"Uh... gud finking Woozy," Catpone acknowledged. "Hey Guts, Uh... button up dem breeches!"

"Yuh mean, batten down dem hatches, Boss... I fink." Gutrumble checked his trouser fly-buttons just in case. "Anyways," he said, spitting out the skin of a well-chewed wriggly and heading below deck with a jar full of them, "I'm expewimenting wiv muh cooking."

"Kicking dem's stupid..." Catpone jumped on the swarm of wrigglies chewing a large circle around him, fell through the hole and lay spread-eagled on the lower deck as Gutrumble trundled down the steps. "Uh, stamping's more afflictive!"

"Effective, boss." Gutrumble flicked a wriggly in the air and caught it in his mouth. "Take muh advice, Boss," he called back to Catpone, casually chewing away as he sauntering towards his kitchen, "use da steps, dey may be slower but dey're considerably less painful!"

"Yuh're afflicted wid idleness, lounging

around duh place at a time like dis! All yuh
ever do is sit on yuh bum! GET UP YUH
LAZY GIT!" ear-bashed Legs, giving
Catpone a kick as she hurried past and up to
the top deck.

Awoo perched on the rigging close to the
twins. "Hasn't Zag got something to get rid
of these things?" he hooted, watching members of the crew pick up buckets full of wrigglies and empty them over the side of the
ship.

Lucy brushed another pile onto William's
shovel. "I hope he'll bring a Thingumma-
gadget to…"

"Sowwy guys but," Spooky looked
anxious as he rushed up to them, "I gotta set
sail befaw duh wrigglies do duh *Mobsea*
terminal damage," he panted, trying to draw
a big breath to shout the order.

"No!" yelled Lucy, "Zag'll have something."

"He's bound to!" said William. "And
anyway, what if they eat the boat while
we're out at sea?"

"Sowwy buh I can't wait no longer!" insisted Spooky, as Legs arrived amongst the bickering.

"What's da pwoblem, my kitties?"

"Tell 'em Legs," Spooky pleaded, "we've gotta set sail before duh wrigglies do duh *Mobsea* terminal dama…"

William suddenly ran off. "I'll be back with something!" he shouted defiantly, heading for the Beamsurfer. He'd figured that even if he missed Zag, the *Mobsea* wouldn't sail without him, and if it did, it would probably sink in the harbour.

Spooky threw his paws up in despair. "Dat's all I need!"

"LOOK OUT! LOOK OUT!" screeched Flewy, zooming across the main deck squawking his head off, closely followed by a large Globolloon which bounced off the masts. Another followed, then another and another as a mass of eerie, dark shapes whooshed past overhead. Everyone dived for cover with the exception of Legs and Lucy. Protected by the rigging they ran to the stern, concerned for William's safety.

"There he is!" shouted Lucy, seeing him running towards the far end of the pontoon.

Legs leapt off the ship and bounded after him like a magnificent tigress, leaving Lucy to gasp in horror at the sight of black, witch-like creatures flying on sticks firing a series of Globolloons at her brother. With relief, she saw William escape the onslaught by jumping from the pontoon on to the sand and taking cover behind a rock.

Four of Gudorphal's Lurkwarriors briefly focused their attention on Legs but her agility was so great that, with her determination to reach William, she dodged and wove out of their way. Hounded by the strange flying creatures, William panicked and broke from cover. He yelled in anguish above the sound of the sea. A massive Globolloon bounced after him, smothering his fearful cries as it enveloped its prey. Legs panted helplessly as it whooshed off into the night sky, but the horror had drawn her attention away from her own safety. Encircled by Lurkwarriors,

she was goaded into swiping out at them with her powerful claws before a final attack. Two large shadows suddenly swooped down amongst them. One went directly for Legs; so swift and deadly was its aim that she was caught up into the sky.

"It's me, Eggna," said the huge eagle. "Gotcha just in time, huh?"

"Just don't dwop me, dat's all," said Legs, grateful but shaken.

Eggna swooped down to the *Mobsea Dick*, concerned to get Legs aboard then rejoin her mate to fight the Lurks. Landing safely on the deck, she released Legs from her grasp and made to take off again. There was no need, Eggbert had already chased off the Lurks and landed alongside her.

"Where's my brother?" shouted Lucy, running towards them as Legs straightened her tattered dress.

"I'm so sowwy my kitty, I weally twied to…"

Lucy burst into floods of tears as Eggna tried to comfort her. "We'll do our very best to find him," she whispered, but Lucy was inconsolable.

Spooky stood close by, aimlessly fiddling with the red bandanna tied around the rim of his trilby. "Don't wuwwy Lucy," he sympathised, feeling he should say something comforting, "I'll 'ave 'em if dey come back."

Catpone had turned the problem into a rare opportunity, taking full advantage of the situation to cuddle Legs. "Yeah we'll uh... PULVERISE dem!"

For once Gutrumble didn't need to correct his boss, the word was well understood by all. With a gesture of grim determination, he hoisted up his belt from around his fat gut. "Wuh can't just stand around doing nuffinck, so I sugg..." he burped, "...est wuh shud sail outta sea an lose ourselves so dey don't find us no more."

"Yeah!" Spooky enthusiastically flipped his trilby back on his head, "an' wuh can get wid of dem wigglies for once an' for all."

"I'll go ahead and warn Astral," said Eggbert, making sure the sky was clear of the invaders. "Sail for the peninsula an' take cover alongside the *Sea Err*'s abandoned carrier-deck. Meet us there," he said, without the slightest inkling that Eraser still existed – let alone had returned to his galleon.

"And please find Zag," Lucy sobbed, keeping close to Eggna.

"PREPARE TO SET SAIL!" Spooky ordered the crew.

"Uh… 'ang on!" said Catpone, more concerned his cuddle times were about to end, "uh… wot if dem uh… fwlying fings uruh 'anging awound out dere waiting tuh uh… ambitious!"

"Ambush us, boss," corrected Gutrumble.

"Yuh duh one being ambitious!" Legs scolded, giving Catpone an indignant shove, "SO GERROFF ME, YA WIMP!"

"SPOOKY!" Awoo suddenly hooted, gaining the mogster's attention. "Zag's Jetticans… Do you still have them?" Until then he'd been racking his brain but feeling useless.

"Dey're still on da stern." Spooky called back. "They'd find it hard to catch us if we use da Jetticans."

"Do you still have the remote control?" Awoo asked, remembering that these power-ful, ozone-friendly, hairspray-sized mini-jet engines had built-in telescopic aerials.

"Yeah, it's still in duh box by da ship's wheel," said Spooky. "HEY! Dat's good finking, Woosy!"

Awoo had felt very woozy when they'd last used them. It was at the time of Eraser's defeat, and the Mogsters had kept fooling around when steering the galleon by the remote control.

"That was a brilliant idea, buddy," Eggbert congratulated Awoo, making him feel very important. "Don't be long!" he added, taking off.

"Waark!" shrieked Flewy, suddenly popping out of an empty fire bucket hanging on a mast, fully goggled, "I'm coming with you!"

"Thanks for your help, Poopadull!" Awoo

shouted, as Flewy chased after Eggbert.

"I hope those Jetticans still work," worried Awoo, flying to the stern to join Spooky.

Evil Eyes

The carrier-deck seemed harmless enough, isolated across the lagoon from the *Sea Err*. Its expanse surprised Zag, being even bigger than he'd expected. Nevertheless this remnant of Eraser's ingenuity sent chills down his spine. It was as if Eraser's presence was still there but, as far as Zag and Astral were concerned, Eraser was no more and that was that.

The breathtaking twin volcanic mountain peaks, though silent in the light of the rising moon, commanded fleeting reflection. Astral sat with Zag in the Beamsurfer and, during such a moment, Zag mentioned the *Sea Err*, further away on their starboard side.

"I tried to persuade the Mogsters to take it over," said Astral, "as a gift for helping us catch Eraser. They couldn't bear to leave the

Mobsea Dick. At least it seems they had the sense to retract the masts and close its submarine canopy across the decks."

"I noticed that as I landed on the carrier-deck," commented Zag, appreciative of such a superb example of invention. "The canopy will help preserve the *Sea Err* until you decide what's to be done with it."

"Probably Spooky saw to that, he is the most sensible out of them," said Astral, as Zag handed the Festalpod to him.

Certain in their own minds that Eraser no longer existed, it was reasonable to assume that the reformed Mogsters had taken such care. To both of them, Eraser's galleon still looked magnificent; having been used as a vessel for evil, it now floated alone and rejected. Enjoying each other's company, neither Zag nor Astral had any idea they were being watched by Eraser and Shystar.

"Looks like a giant chrysalis," said Zag, pointing to the rings which spiralled to the tapered end of the crusty brown Festalpod.

"It has a very similar function," said

Astral, examining it. "The rings act like a thread on a screw, that's how it locks into the Juvitree."

"Why is it removable?" asked Zag. "I thought it had always to remain in the Juvitree?"

"Once a season – but only for a very brief moment – the Rutilan man and wife, the caretakers, would remove it and rinse it in the lake, to rid the Festalpod of any impurities," replied Astral.

"You mentioned the Juvitree when we spoke on the Cosmoputa. For the moment I'm at a loss as to what all of this means exactly," smiled Zag. "But with respect, if the Festalpod and Telijencia are so important, why is it only now that you have become so concerned?"

"Fair question and I will answer that first," said Astral. "We have always been concerned and searched avidly for it, as I told you. However, the events which occurred as a result of Eraser stealing the Orb of Brilliance, prevented us from maintaining a constant search."

"But surely you would have experienced at least some bad effects from the loss of the Festalpod and Telijencia?" Zag queried.

"That is what's so odd," said Astral. "Creativity has slowed down and new advancements are not being made as quickly as they should be, but there has not been anything of real threat so far."

"Whoever's stolen Telijencia is either careless in losing the Festalpod or has no clue as to the island's power," remarked Zag. "But is it possible to steal an island?"

"Well, it is missing," replied Astral, "and the Festalpod turning up proves Telijencia still exists somewhere. If it's not returned, every galaxy throughout the universe will stagnate and rot in the pollution of bad ideas. If Eraser had ever got his hands on the Festalpod he'd have been in his evil element and we wouldn't be here now."

"Perish the thought!" said Zag. "So tell me about the island – its ecology and purpose?"

"I can do better than that, I'll show you," smiled Astral, handing the Festalpod back to Zag. "That's if you don't mind me using your Cosmoputa."

"Of course not," replied Zag, "I'll put this back in the bag, it's still slimy."

Astral took a small golden box from out of his white cloak. Inside was an emerald-green jewel, which he placed in the centre of the vista-globe. For a moment it twirled suspended in the purple haze, then burst into scenes of Telijencia as it once was.

Zag watched and listened intently and full of wonder as Astral began to show him Telijencia and its Lake of Forgotten Ideas.

Lush with vegetation, a range of mountains circled the island. On the outer edge were golden tropical beaches caressed by a deep blue sea. Inland, the circular mountain range formed a bowl with the shores of the great lake, the heart of the island. Through forest glades, streams could be seen feeding rivers, which in turn fed huge waterfalls that gushed down the sides of cliffs.

Astral pointed to a deep, narrow gorge.
"That is the only entry point to the great lake.

"So it's made up of sea water?" Zag queried.

"Not all the time. That is one of the island's natural wonders," said Astral. "The gorge slides shut with the same effect as the lock-gates on a canal. It only opens briefly after the Vernal Eclipse and the period of rejuvenation have passed, to allow the sea salt to cleanse the lake of any impurities."

"That's amazing," Zag gasped. "But what is...?"

"The Vernal Eclipse," said Astral, anticipating the question, "is when the Crystal Planet of Cyan from the Constellation of Colour passes across the face of the sun, making it glow green. It happens..." Astral paused, "in your world I'd say with equivalent frequency to your every springtime."

Zag continued to watch and listen as Astral drew his attention to some rocks near the edge of the lake.

"Somewhere near those rocks stands the putrefied stump of the dormant Juvitree. The Festalpod should be sitting in the centre of the stump and linked to the taproot of the Juvitree. At every Vernal Eclipse, when the sun glows green, the protruding Festalpod shudders into life. This makes the lake erupt into a gigantic fountain in the shape of a tornado, whirling high into the sky. This fountain creates a torrential idea-storm which rains upon the whole island."

"What sort of ideas?" asked Zag.

"Those which cannot be recalled," replied Astral. "For example, those moments of inspiration when you wake in the middle of the night with an idea but go back to sleep and can't remember it in the morning."

"I know they end up in Telijencia, but how?" Zag was very intrigued.

"It's simpler than you think," Astral smiled. "As soon as ideas are mislaid, they drift into the Galaxy of Ideas. For a while they float around, waiting to be remembered. Those which are truly forgotten build up into a huge pool of ideas, which in fact is the great lake."

Zag could hardly believe that such a beautiful island could be lost.

"So how are the ideas recycled for other minds to think of them?" Zag asked, as the pictures in the vista-globe came to an end.

Astral put the emerald jewel back into its box. "In the aftermath of the storm, tranquillity springs forth and, with a flourish, the Juvitree awakens and grows lush, tropical, petal-like leaves which form a rich green and golden crown. They energise the Festalpod at the centre of the stump, then the rejuvenation season of spawning begins."

"Spawning?"

"Deep in the Juvitree's taproot lives the Juvi-beestle."

"Juvi-beestle?"

Astral explained. "A grublike creature that looks like a cross between a very long thin squid and a beautifully coloured sea-slug with orange, blue and white tufted gills. It awakes from hibernation, injecting many thousands of tiny eggs into the Festalpod."

"Incredible," said Zag, as Astral handed the Festalpod back to him.

Astral nodded in agreement. "Nurtured inside the Festalpod, the eggs hatch into blue and white-striped Beetapillars which swarm over the island in their masses. Feeding ravenously on the globules waiting on the lush vegetation as a result of the torrential idea-storm, they rapidly increase in size until their skins burst."

"Their skins burst?"

"That's another wonder," said Astral. "Their metamorphosis is complete and they emerge as exotic Beautiflies."

"How fantastic!" Zag looked at the Festalpod in wonder. "It's similar to how caterpillars turn into butterflies."

"Only these," Astral smiled enthusiastically, "emerge with silken wings which bedazzle you with their festivity of colours as they buzz with rejuvenated ideas."

"How are the ideas redistributed?"

"A rainbow touches the Juvitree

signifying that all is at peace, and the season of rejuvenation is over. From all across the island the Beautiflies return to the Juvitree, swarm into the rainbow and migrate to the Constellation of Colour, the place from where every rainbow is sent. It is by these means that the ideas are redistributed into the Galaxy of Ideas for the benefit of all creativity."

Zag's fascination suddenly turned to alarm. "But, if everything's so vital to the rejuvenation process, what's happened now the Festalpod's missing from the island?"

"Without it the lake will become stagnant, making Telijencia a slime-ridden, putrid place." Astral went silent for a brief moment. "Who knows what dangers will be lurking on there?"

"WAAAARK," shrieked Flewy, as both he and Eggbert swooped onto the carrier-deck. "William's been snatched in a huge balloon... there're weird things flying about like giant slugs on sticks... a...and... Legs got..."

"Okay, let's take this slowly," said Zag, quickly jumping out of the Beamsurfer with Astral, not understanding what Flewy was trying to say.

"If it wasn't for Eggbert... or was it Eggna...? then I don't know what..."

"Just calm down while Eggbert tells us," said Astral.

"CALM DOWN!" screeched Flewy, "we've got no time to BE CALM!"

"Well do it anyway," said Zag, firmly.

Eggbert clearly and succinctly described what had happened: William's fate and Lucy's complete distress at the loss of her brother. As they listened Zag stood horrified and Astral's youthful-looking face filled with anxiety.

With difficulty, Zag kept his self-control. He knew it was absolutely vital not to panic – that would only make things far worse. Reaching inside his Thingummajacket for his Cosmo-fob, he hoped to contact William. Holding it in the palm of his hand, he mind-activated the device. But instead of the vista-globe bursting out like a fountain of stardust, it struggled to appear and no communication was made. "Where's Lucy?" he asked, about to try to contact her.

"On the *Mobsea Dick* with Eggna and the rest," replied Eggbert. "They're sailing here to take cover alongside you. I thought the Carrier's size would protect them from being attacked on all sides and they'd be less vulnerable."

"They could be at greater risk at sea!" said Astral, gravely concerned.

"It's okay, they'll be here soon," said Eggbert. "Awoo had the great idea of using the Jetticans."

"I've got to go, they should have been here by now!" said Zag, extremely worried. "The jet-propulsion granules in those aerosols are old, not long-life, and are out of the batch I brought the very first time we met the Mogsters."

"SEE! " squawked Flewy, "Twit-Head's not had a sensible idea in his life."

"No time for your nonsense, Flewy!" Zag

put his Cosmo-fob inside his Thingumma-jacket. "I have to protect Lucy and somehow find William."

Astral placed a comforting hand on Zag's shoulder. "I'll go to my Master and summon my Defenders. We'll do everything in our power to help find William."

"I'll go with Zag," said Eggbert.

Zag smiled warmly at the eagle. "I'd appreciate that, but hurry up," he said, jumping aboard the Beamsurfer.

"DON'T FORGET ME!" squawked Flewy, flying aboard the craft and shoving his way past Eggbert.

"Keep in contact on the Cosmoputa," suggested Astral, "so my Defenders and I can co-ordinate our search with you." He stood a little way from the Beamsurfer and held up his pendant of infinity. A breeze ruffled his hair and the white cloak around his tall slim figure as a golden sphere of light appeared in front of him, like a bolt from the blue. "KEEP CONTACT AND STAY SAFE!" he called out. Stepping inside his sphere, Astral was whisked away like a comet in the heavens.

"Don't say that smelly thing's still in here!" said Flewy, seeing the Festalpod protruding out of the bag on his seat and kicking it onto the floor.

"That's the least of our worries," said Zag, about to close the cockpit door.

"YUCKY!' Flewy shrieked, "One's come out of Gutrumble's 'keepsick'!"

Eggbert snapped up the lonesome wriggly in his beak and chucked it out of the door. "These things ain't right either, that's for sure," said Eggbert.

"Even I know that, stupid," squawked Flewy rudely. "We'll end up inside balloons or be eaten to death by black wrigglies with sharp teeth and that grow so big they should POP!"

Eggbert glared, "Shut ya rudeness down pal..."

"I bet they even turn into flying slugs, bit like you only without feathers," quipped Flewy.

"...BEFORE I EAT YA!" the eagle continued, beak to beak with Flewy.

Zag was too deep in thought and far too concerned to take any notice of Flewy's behaviour. He closed the door, made sure all seat belts were fastened, then the Cosmoputa burst into life and the Beamsurfer took off. "Maybe the wrigglies aren't the least of our worries!" he thought, changing his mind. He was still unaware of the ever-watchful eyes from across the lagoon, aboard the ghostly *Sea Err*.

"Dive! Dive! DIVE!" shouted Eraser, gleefully back in action, anticipating a secure evil future, with his galleon fully honed into the location of the *Mobsea Dick* about two kilometres away. In submarine mode, masts retracted and canopy closed, the *Sea Err* was as sleek as a tuna fish, and made incredibly swift headway underwater.

"WE CAN GO FASTER THAN THIS!" yelled Shystar, taking to his new role as easily as a duck takes to water.

"YOU TELL 'EM!" bawled Eraser, manically jumping up and down on his poop-deck. In sheer vanity, he delighted at the reflection of his new pirate attire as the water raced passed the watertight transparent canopy. Stopping to flick a heel and admire his pristine black buckled boots, he grabbed Shystar and stuck his nose-boil straight in the Eradicator's face. "You're doing well, but don't ever try doing TOO well!" he spat. "ALWAYS remember, NOBODY MESSES with ERASER THE TERRIBLE! Including ZAG and his friends – they're going to SUFFER my revenge TOO!"

Zag took the Beamsurfer high into the sky to gain a more expansive view of the sea. "How many wrigglies did you see, Flewy?"

"Only thousands, sorry if I didn't count them accurately!" Flewy answered sarcastically. "STREWTH! They're only infesting the whole blooming island! Anyway, you just told me they're the least of our..."

"Vista-mail to Astral," said Zag, dictating a message to the Cosmoputa as he sped towards the Mobsea Dick.

"I am concerned that the sudden appearance of the Festalpod is the cause of William's capture. Also that it's possible the Festalpod has spawned mutant caterpillars. I recall Legs telling me, before you and I met on the carrier, that this was the first time these so-called wrigglies have infested this island. I think whoever stole the Festalpod are the attackers and will do anything to get it back! They also might well know the plight of Telijencia – End of message from your good friend, Zagwitz."

The Vortex

The *Mobsea Dick* had made quick passage out to sea but had lost its course owing to the failing and spluttering Jetticans. Way off the coastline, the Mogsters' galleon bobbed up, down and around, sailing in fits and starts. Under the circumstances neither Awoo nor Spooky fancied being exposed to further attacks from the dark flying beasts and their 'balloons', by messing about over the stern of the ship. They had wondered if the remote controller was the problem – it was the easier to access but far too complex a device to fiddle with. Fortunately they had a sudden wave of common sense and decided to put up with the jolting and leave well alone. With the wriggly infestation having subsided, apart from those stored in jars by Gutrumble to further develop his culinary skills, there was not much to do except hope the ship would go faster.

Gutrumble stumbled up to the quarter-deck feeling seasick and it wasn't because he'd tried eating the sac-bodied translucent creatures which were now bursting out of the wrigglies. They were less chewy than their grown-up counterparts that he had hanging around his belt. "Spooky, I feel pukey," he shouted, throwing up near the ship's wheel.

"Yeah, uh... why are we going 'wound in uhhhhh... cycles," heaved Catpone, making it a technicolour duet.

"C...cccircles, Bosssss," puked Gutrumble. "Fwarrr, dat one stinks!"

"If wuh weren't, wuh are now," yelped Spooky, jumping away from the gut-rendering deluge, leaving the wheel to spin wildly.

"Why dus sicky always 'ave carrots in it?" rasped Gutrumble, looking positively green and inspecting his performance, "Wuh don' evun eat 'em."

"Stop messing about," Awoo hooted,

perched on the mizzen-boom out of splash range and unaware of his understatement. "If it wasn't for Lucy I'd have flown off here by now, we need to get to the shelter of the *Carrier!*" He flew down to the main deck to see how Lucy was getting on. The *Sea Err* itself was much closer than he could ever have imagined and for all the wrong reasons – even its periscope was already firmly focused on the *Mobsea Dick*.

Lucy was searching her pockets for a handkerchief and her sobbing face suddenly lit up. She took out the Cosmo-fob which in all the commotion and her anxiety she had completely forgotten. Keeping the crystal upwards in the palm of her hand she shut her eyes.

"What's that?" asked Awoo, grateful that Eggna was staying with Lucy.

"I'm trying to contact William," Lucy replied excitedly, concentrating on the Cosmo-fob. Taking Awoo and Eggna by surprise, a vista-globe burst out of the Cosmo-fob then flickered to nothing.

"William, talk to me!" she shouted desperately.

Without warning the *Mobsea Dick* came under attack from hoards of Lurkwarriors. The frenzied, dark shapes appeared as if from nowhere, darting to and fro on their slither-sticks around and above the galleon as Gudorphal directed his ruthless action. Globolloons rained heavily onto the ship, this time with greater force. As the foremast and bowsprit splintered under the strain, the Lurkwarriors encircled the galleon like Red Indians terrorising a wagon-train. Flying faster and faster, they became first a blur, then a seemingly solid ring of blackness, whipping the sea into a frenzy. Helplessly caught in the grip of this gigantic whirlpool, the *Mobsea Dick* sped in ever decreasing circles. All aboard were flung to the port side by the centrifugal force and Lucy lost hold of the Cosmo-fob.

High in the sky, Eggbert sat beside Zag, scanning the expanse of ocean with his keen eyes. But it was Flewy's goggles which reaped their reward; he was the first to spot them. "I can see them! I can see them!" he squawked.

"They're under some sort of attack!" said Eggbert, trying to make out what was happening.

The Beamsurfer started to speed towards the ailing *Mobsea Dick*. It was not Zag's doing. Realising the craft was going out of control, he fought with the joystick then pressed the reverse-thrust booster-button on the control panel. But for their safety belts, they'd have been bashed about inside the craft like loose eggs in a bucket belted by a thunderbolt.

Beads of perspiration ran down Zag's face as he managed to equalise the colossal gravitational pull towards the sea. High above the turmoil, the Beamsurfer hovered precariously as Zag focused his telescope on the *Mobsea Dick*.

"If ya go any closer we'll be sucked in!" Eggbert gasped anxiously, seeing the ship hopelessly caught in the violent swirling sea.

Zag constantly countered the drag as best he could. They watched helplessly as the *Mobsea Dick* swirled ever closer to the centre of the violent whirlpool and entered its doom.

"Look, there's Eggna!" shrieked Flewy.

"Hey yeah, pal," Eggbert shouted excitedly, "an' she's got Lucy in her talons... an' Lucy's holding Awoo!"

As Zag tried to adjust the telescope for a better close-up, the *Mobsea Dick* and the Lurkwarriors disappeared into the gaping black hole at the centre of the vortex. They watched Eggna bravely fight against the drag. One second she was there – desperately clutching onto Lucy and Awoo – then they were gone.

"Let's get out of here!" screeched Flewy, as the force of the gravitational pull gave a final determined invitation for the Beamsurfer to join the fateful party.

Zag frantically pushed at buttons, flicked switches and rotated the joystick. Flewy and Eggbert hung grimly to their seat belts as he desperately struggled with the controls. At maximum reverse thrust, the gauge had already well passed red and something had to give way. Sparks flew around the cockpit as all the dials spun in a frenzied blur; the Cosmoputa's vista-globe popped and crackled with fuzz then went completely blank.

Completely out of control, the craft spiralled downwards to the awesome dark vortex of the ocean swirling tunnel. With a massive jolt of turbulence the Beamsurfer and its hapless crew disappeared as if sucked down a giant plug-hole – into the depths of the unknown.

Lying in Wait

Eraser had commanded the *Sea Err* to dive into the core of the vortex at the precise moment the Lurkwarriors created the whirlpool. He had no worries, to his beloved *Sea Err* such an ordeal was less of a problem than squashing an ant with a sledgehammer.

Succeeding in being the first to arrive at the Lake of Forgotten Ideas, his sinister galleon lay silent below the surface.

Shystar searched busily through a drawer as Eraser sat at his antique desk, peering at the large screen revealed from behind his cabin's wood panelling. A small dot flashed on the screen, making a series of bleeps.

"HURRY UP!" Eraser barked irritably. "It's there somewhere!"

"They're not clearly labelled, SAR!" Shystar rummaged through another set of spectra-maps, each the size of a small thermometer. "Looks like the *Mobsea's* here though."

"Don't state the obvious!" Eraser bawled. "FIND ME THAT SPECTRA-MAP OF TELIJENCIA!"

"Ah, this may be it, Sar!" Shystar held it up to the lantern chandelier then helpfully blew some dust off it.

"Blowing it won't make it work, YOU IDIOT!" Eraser grabbed the crystalnode and inserted it into the control-panel's spectra-drive. It flickered a weak yellowish glow. "IT'S NOT WORKING!" he raved, banging his fist on the control panel. The spectra-map sparked into life shining bright ice-blue and the screen displayed how Telijencia used to be.

"I wonder if that pair of Rutilans are still here, Sar?" queried Shystar, spotting the plan of a cottage on the hilly wooded slopes above the side of the lake. "Didn't they look after the Juvitree and supply you with duff ideas?"

"THEY DID!" shouted Eraser, annoyed at being reminded of how they took him for a complete fool before he finally managed to break away from the Master and steal the Orb of Brilliance. "AND BE SURE THEY'LL PAY FOR THAT IF THEY ARE HERE!" Like a concert pianist striking the first note, he smugly tapped the focus-button to search the area of the lake for the *Mobsea Dick*. Immediately the small dot flashed, indicating it was a kilometre away. Eraser smirked, "AT LAST! THOSE MANKY FURBALLS HAVEN'T A CLUE what power they've on board their HEAP of a galleon!"

Shystar coughed nervously, "Uhmm Sar, you sure the Festalpod's aboard the *Mobsea Dick*?"

"NOT THE POINT!" bellowed Eraser, scanning the map.

"Shystar looked amazed at such a reply. "B…but… what if…?"

"THAT'S the key to our success!" Eraser cackled, "BECAUSE albeit for very different reasons," he said, picking his nose, "WHO-EVER has it, wants to put it back right there!" He gleefully excavated a greeny, flicked it directly at the screen and bogied the location of the Juvitree. "AND THAT INCLUDES US!"

"But Sar, that's my point," Shystar urged. "As the Mogsters don't know what it's for, we must get it off them straightaway in case they get rid of it."

"I'll leave the Lurks to sort them out!" Eraser barked, feeling clever. He studied their position on the map in relation to the Juvitree intently.

Shystar looked even more astounded. "B...but... but?"

"STOP DOING MY THINKING!" Eraser shouted angrily, getting up from his desk and stomping to his wardrobe. "TAKE THESE!" he yelled, pulling out a box of Defender uniforms left over from the time before he and his men became traitors. "YOU and SIX Eradicators get into them PRON-TO! Make ready my Camersible launch...

AND WEAR THE HELMETS... THAT MINI-SUB'S NOT GOT MUCH HEAD-ROOM!"

Eraser grimaced as he quickly changed into his own Defender uniform, having always thought himself far too talented for such a role. It was still oversized for his scrawny figure and its black colour had faded in places. This was the last thing he'd ever wanted to wear again but he knew such deception could prove vital. Taking off his large gold hooped earring, he went to tuck his frizzy ginger mane of hair into the helmet but it hissed like a snake. "WHAT THE...?" he yelled, dropping it like a red-hot potato. Tentatively kicking it to see what would pop out, he noticed the small button on the helmet's ear-piece and realised he'd accidentally pressed the receptor-speaker button. "Bit primitive, but could be handy!" he muttered, checking his pockets to see if the standard-issue miniature microphone was still in the old uniform. He didn't bother even to glance in his splendid mirror to preen himself. None the wiser as to his appearance, he hurriedly left his cabin looking like he'd put a saucepan on his head, with his long hooked nose protruding like a bent handle.

"STOP GAWPING!" Eraser bawled as he joined Shystar and the selected Eradicators at the bow of the submerged *Sea Err*, "AND GET IN!"

The watertight hatch was already open with retractable steps lowered into the prepared and waiting Camersible. This sleek, but cleverly compact, stingray-like amphibious submarine was armed with a flash lens in the nose-cone, and was just as deadly as its 'close relation' the Cameracraft. On each side the fins streamlined into a triangular canopied module containing three rows of seats – two in front for the pilot and co-pilot with two rows of three directly behind.

With all aboard and Shystar sitting next to him, Eraser closed the canopy, signalling the watertight launch hatch to be flooded by some of the remaining Eradicators. A section of the *Sea Err*'s bow opened, releasing the craft like a whale giving birth to its baby. The Camersible sped stealthily underwater towards the bank of the lake by the Juvitree. Free once more and excited by the prospect of action, the Eradicators chattered expectantly.

"SHUT UP AND LISTEN!" bellowed Eraser, slowing down the craft. "We ambush the Lurks as soon as they put the Festalpod in the Juvitree. THEY MUST NOT be allowed to remove it! TELIJEN-CIA MUST REJUVENATE for me to take control of all the ideas!" He pressed a tab, raising the aerial-like periscopic camera to make sure all was clear.

The Camersible emerged from the stagnant lake and sneaked its way up the bank like a foraging monster clam. Leaving two Eradicators in control of the craft, Eraser, Shystar and the other four quickly jumped out.

"Go a little way off, submerge and wait for our signal," Shystar ordered, before following the others.

The steamy, greenish-grey atmosphere reminded Eraser, from his days as a Defender, that the season of the Vernal Eclipse was due. He took the tiny microphone from his pocket, placed it at the base of the Juvitree then hurried to take cover nearby, smirking in the knowledge that it wouldn't be long before he took over Telijencia.

"That lake stinks!" said one of the Eradicators, following the others behind a cluster of rotting giant fungi.

"Yeah, those Lurks have made a right mess of this place!" agreed another.

Eraser turned around. "I've already told you lot to shut up!" he barked, just as he lost his footing on the slimy surface and fell headlong onto a large jagged rock. To his surprise it was soft and squidgy. Repulsed by the oozing membranous texture, he shivered with dread as he realised the cesspitial world of Lurkamungoo could not be far away. Eraser heard a squelching noise and shuddered at the thought of the gurgle-sucking Putrisphere.

"Something's by the Juvitree!" an Eradicator suddenly warned, making Eraser nearly jump out of his skin.

Shystar snatched the telescope out of the Eradicator's hand. "It's those Rutilans with two kids, Sar."

"TWO kids?" Eraser grabbed the telescope. "Now that is handy," he leered. "Let's get them!"

"Wait!" Shystar tugged at Eraser's arm. "Look up there – Lurks!"

Eraser pushed Shystar aside but instead of bawling him out for being insolently tactile, his concentration became fixed on the hoard of Lurkwarriors landing on the slippery bank of the lake. As if completely demented, he started bashing both sides of his helmet with the flat of his hands. "That stupid microphone can't be working!"

"My receptor's tuned in and working," said Shystar. "Maybe you haven't switched yours on properly, Sar."

Eraser gritted his teeth and whispered harshly, "I'm not stupid, you..." Fiddling with a small button on his helmet's ear-piece, he discovered Shystar to be correct. "Tune your receptors, you dim-wits!" he ordered.

"Are you there, Sar?" said a voice through the receptor.

"Now everybody wants to chat!" Eraser ranted, just managing to keep his voice low. "Who's that anyway?"

"The Camersible," said the voice. "The Lurks are flying towards you."

"I know that already, you idiot!" Eraser snarled, "SO BOG OFF. I'm trying to listen to what's going on here!"

"Remain silent until we call you," added Shystar.

"I've already told them that!" Eraser whisper-ranted, watching the Rutilans standing patiently by the Juvitree.

Some of the Lurkwarriors took to bathing in the stagnant lake, 'refreshing' themselves from the residue of itchy sea-salt that clung to their skin as a result of their foray to the Island of Radiance. Even so they appeared to be waiting for something.

Interrogutted

Putridia had argued incessantly that they should first return to Lurkamungoo to check out their globollised captive. Her nagging had merely fuelled Gudorphal's obstinacy until she suggested it could prove worthwhile to interrogate the unfortunate and confirm the Festalpod was aboard the *Mobsea Dick*.

Having conceded, Gudorphal decided it prudent to send Malodour and the majority of the Lurkwarriors to wait for him and Putridia on the opposite banks of the great lake by the Juvitree. Selecting a dozen to accompany them, Gudorphal, Putridia and the small group of slobbery followers whooshed on their slithersticks through a boggy vortex and down into Lurkamungoo.

The putrid walls and ceilings of the goo-ridden dank cavern bubbled with obnoxious bursts, like a plague of well-overgrown, festering boils. William's Globolloon hung luminous green in the conical roof. Horrid squeak-gurgling Globlins, each no larger than a football and made of rancid snotty-green jelly, splurtle-sprung from the pulsating ceiling and clung to the Globolloon. Their stubby tentacles held boney-sticks with which they relentlessly prodded the Globolloon to torment William into activity and make it glow brighter. Shouting as loudly as possible, William punched and kicked, desperately trying to knock his tormentors off his prison's translucent rubbery skin. Once more he tried in vain to contact Zag on the Cosmo-fob but, as many times before, the vista-globe sparkled then fizzled to nothing.

"That's enough," shouted Gudorphal, signalling the Lurkwarriors to chase the Globlin-fiends away. Screeching like hyenas, they disappeared into the membraned, honeycomb-shaped cavities, which splurted them into the dense fungi jungle above.

"So let's see what we is having here!" Putridia dribbled excitedly. Expanding the tentacle out of her forehead, she pointed a sucker-like finger and squirted a bright orange liquid directly at the Globolloon.

With a loud pop, William fell down onto a spongy bed of ponging, dark-green viscous slime. Appalled at the repulsive bog-eyed, mucus-dripping creatures, he lay clinging tightly to the Cosmo-fob concealed in his hand.

"Welcome to Lurkamungoo!" Putridia slobber-cackled.

"LEAVE ME ALONE!" he yelled, as Putridia prodded him with her slitherstick to make him stand up. Recognising the Lurkwarriors, he sensibly recalled how his run of panic had led to his capture in the first place. William stood in dread, trying to overcome his fear and not make matters worse. He trembled at the thought of what horrors lay in store.

"Yooze not one of those cat-pirates!" slurped Gudorphal, rather disappointed.

"It's a KIDDYBEEN," splurted Putridia happily, "oozling with energy!"

"Never mind about that," Gudorphal spittled, wanting to get straight to the point with William. "Is the Festalpod aboard the *Mobsea Dick?*"

"P...pardon?" stuttered William, wondering how to answer in a way that would allow him time to think.

"Polite too," slurped Putridia. "Might keep yooze as a mascot."

"Now there's an offer!" grin-spewed Gudorphal. "You see, we might go easy on you if you tell us."

"I... I was trying to escape from them," William suddenly found himself saying, "so I don't know."

"So yooze were," Putridia gummy-slobbered, "from a big cat-pirate in a funny dress."

"IN THAT CASE," gob-mouthed Gudorphal, "THIS IS A COMPLETE WASTE OF TIME!"

Putridia pointed her slitherstick at

William. "Sorry but you's of no use to us... byzeee... b..."

"WAIT!" shouted William, "I CAN be of help!" His last adventure on the one-time island of Blot ,when locked in the hold of the *Mobsea Dick* with Lucy, Awoo and Legs, had taught William to always keep his wits about him.

"HOW?" splurted Putridia, stopping the Globolloon forming and letting the snotty-green ooze drip from her slitherstick's flared, trumpet-like end.

"What did you say you're looking for?" asked William politely, although he knew full well.

"OUR FESTALPOD!" splurted Gud-orphal in frustration. "YOOZE whittling our time. Globollise HIM!"

"I CAN HELP!" yelled William. "I was confused, that's all, because I thought it was the cat-pirate's ship you were after."

"Give the lad a chance you bully-aching SO-AND-SO!" gob-splurted Putridia.

"Thank you, ma'am," said William.

"YOU IS SO polite," giggled Putridia, slobbering a gummy smile.

"I need to know what this Fes... fes..."

"FESTALPOD!" splattered Gudorphal, "AND GET ON WITH WHAT YOU IS TELLING!"

"...Festalpod looks like," said William, playing for time to prepare his escape plan.

"Like a very big chrysalis," slurped Putridia.

"As in butterfly?" queried William, clinging in blind faith to his Cosmo-fob. It hadn't been able to make contact inside the Globolloon but maybe... just maybe...

"ONLY MUCH BIGGER!" splurted Gudorphal. He was more and more tempted to globollise William and have done with it.

William held the Cosmo-fob in the palm of his hand and wished hard to hide himself. The vista-globe sparked into life – the Chameleoniser function worked at last. For a moment Gudorphal and Putridia, wobbled splutter-smacked.

"YOOZE AND YOOZE STUPID

IDEAS!" blubber-bawled Gudorphal.

William used the dimness of the cavern to his advantage, at the same time remembering that any fast movement could give him away. But the over-heated argument that ensued between Gudorphal and Putridia helped greatly to divert their attention. On all fours, like a soldier at war, William crawled to take cover behind a huge mound of spongy slime. Little did he know that hidden underneath lay the wrecked Cameracraft that belonged to Eraser.

"HE CAN'T ESCAPE OUT OF HERE OR TELIJENCIA!" splurted Gudorphal, as Putridia fussed about trying to direct the Lurkwarriors in a search. "WE'S WILL DEAL WITH THIS MATTER LATER!"

Gudorphal mounted his slitherstick and ordered Putridia and the Lurkwarriors to follow him. William watched them whoosh through a flapping, ooze-dripping, membranous vent high up in the cavern's wall.

Now it was a case of what he should do next!

Held for Ransom

The Eradicators pulled out their flashguns and aimed them at Putridia and Gudorphal, as they whooshed down to land next to the four Rutilans like gruesome giant festering lollipops dripping on sticks.

"Don't zap them 'till I say so!" ordered Eraser, fine-tuning his helmet's ear-piece receptor.

Malodour joined Putridia and Gudorphal by the stump of the Juvitree. "The Lurkwarriors is getting all restless," he slurped.

"They'snot got business t'be restless!" Gudorphal splurted angrily. "They's mutants and wouldn't be existing if it wasn't for us!"

"Exactly," splattered Putridia. "Anyways, we's been busy with other pressing matters." She nonchalantly flicked her tendrilous hair with a tentacle. "Still think we should've searched for that boy we captured."

"So you keep saying and yooze is getting boring," Gudorphal slurped. "He'll be globollised with the others when we capture them. So that's that!"

"What boy? Maybe those Rutilans have more than two," Eraser theorised, as he and his men concentrated on every movement, more than prepared to ambush the Lurks at any moment.

Shystar ordered the Camersible to be ready to zap any Lurkwarriors that tried to escape. "It's very odd, Sar," he whispered, "they don't seem to be taking much notice of the Rutilans."

"It's not odd, you idiot, it's obvious," Eraser replied gruffly. "The Rutilans are under Gudorphal's control."

Gudorphal pointed a sucker across the rancid lake. "Those cat-pirates s'not going nowhere," he jelly-wobbled proudly, "the

Festalpod's on their galleon, their galleon's somewhere on this lake, SO LET'S FIND IT!"

Putridia pointed to the Rutilans. "What about those pathetic cretins?" she chuckle-wobbled scornfully.

"Keep a look out for our return or yooze'll be globollised too!"Gudorphal snarled at them. "And make sure yooze hands are really glowing because we's wanting big burly Festalmaggots."

"Mr Presidumpt," creep-seeped Malodour, "shall I gives out the order for the Lurkwarriors to search for the galleon?"

"Yes Mr Slime Minister," chuckle-slurped Gudorphal. "We'll pummel their ship with Globolloons, break the masts so they're not protected by the rigging, then we'll globollise them."

Having unexpectedly been promoted, Malodour was determined not to let this task go awry. "Slithersticks at the ready!" he splurted at the Lurkwarriors, "LET'S GO!"

Eraser made sure all the Lurks had gone, then ordered his Eradicators to surround the Rutilans. "VERY LONG TIME NO SEE!" Eraser bawled, confronting the astounded foursome. "IF IT ISN'T MY OLD FRIENDS EILRA AND NALA!" Eraser took off his helmet and inspected them. "Aren't you unlucky, first the Lurks and now ME!" He grinned manically. "Come, come now, at least be polite and introduce me to your brats!" He peered with incredulity at the short, but very tubby, bedraggled wretches who wore identical green, gunge-dripping, plastic-type macintoshes which were two sizes too small. Their small heads and protruding ears looked lost under their floppy caps.

Nala pulled them close to her. "Th...thay b...be our offspring."

"Yeah, they look like kangaroos," Eraser sneered, flicking his gloved fingers for Shystar to grab the two offspring and set them apart from their parents.

"Y...you th...thum thar leave thum alone,

thay ain't done nuffing, so thay 'aven't!"
shouted Eilra.

"That's true," Eraser said softly. "BUT
YOU HAVE!" he yelled, "AND NOBODY
MESSES WITH ME!"

"Y...yah can't treat us like this, yur a
D...Defender," Nala quivered.

"Oh dear, I nearly forgot," Eraser cackled
sarcastically, conducting the Eradicators to
join in his amusement. "It's a long story and
you don't have to worry about such a small
matter. BUT YOU DO HAVE TO BE
VERY WORRIED ABOUT ME!" He
pulled out his flashgun and zapped the offspring, capturing them into its light. Nala
collapsed in Eilra's quivering arms. "Comfort
them in your nice way!" sneered Eraser,
ejecting the prismatran and giving it to
Shystar.

"You can see it if you wish, they look
sorta cute," smiled Shystar, showing the
pathetic faces frozen inside the prismatran.
"The good news is," he smiled, "we can bring
them back any time we want. But you must

tell us everything you know and do exactly as Eraser says... However if you don't..."

"W...we will furr sure, so be it," stammered Eilra, holding onto Nala.

"Cheer up," Shystar smiled sweetly, "things are getting better already."

"Not quite!" Eraser sneered, taking the prismatran off Shystar. "They need to convince me they'll co-operate and not waste my time like before."

"We jus' said we will, what more d'yar want?" pleaded Nala.

Eraser stooped and peered in her eyes. "How many kids do you have?"

"T...two, jus' thar two," she stuttered.

"Then who's the boy the Lurks have captured?" Eraser asked, smugly.

"An'ow arr we supos'd ta know thart, so we don't!" replied Eilra.

"I'VE NO MORE TIME TO WASTE HERE!" bawled Eraser. "DESTROY THE PRISMATR..."

"NO!" pleaded Nala. "All we know's we found an eagle, a girl and an owl when collecting spores," she blurted anxiously. "They're at our cottage resting thar energy 'cos thar young un's in a dre'ful state."

A knowing, evil grin spewed across Eraser's pallid features. "You'd better go back and look after them WELL!" he barked. "And show no sign of upset or betray me," he added, menacingly holding up the prismatran. "NOT YOU!" he shouted, grabbing Eilra as Nala scuttled back to her cottage on the slopes.

Shystar fidgeted. "Better get under cover

in case the Lurks return."

Eraser seized Eilra, roughly ushering him behind a pulsating rock, and interrogated him, whilst Shystar sent the Eradicators back into their positions.

"THIS MORON," Eraser ranted at Shystar as he rejoined them, "DID A DEAL WITH THE LURKS AT MY EXPENSE!"

"B...but I thum thar 'ad to, they wurr goin' to globollise Nala," trembled Eilra. "They stole her from me, so t'was!"

"SO WHAT!" Eraser yelled, "THEY NICKED the Festalpod. NOW I'VE NICKED YOUR KIDS AND NOW YOU DO WHAT I SAY!"

"B...bu... but..."

"DON'T YOU 'BUT' ME!" Eraser raved, "YOU CAUSED ME HEAPS OF PROBLEMS, YOU HALF-BAKED NERD! You LET the Lurks TAKE control! THEN THEY SUCKED Telijencia to the Galaxy of INCOGNITO where EVERY-THING disappears AND EVEN I COULD-N'T FIND IT!"

"I'm thum thar very sorry, so I am," quaked Eilra, nodding in pathetic desperation to emphasise his utter repentance.

"I think he's very sorry," mocked Shystar.

"That's okay then," Eraser said softly. "SORRY!" he raved. "Listen, you LITTLE SQUIRT! With an eagle, a girl, an owl and a boy stuck in a Globolloon, I've every reason to believe a WHITE-BEARDED ODD-BALL is on this island, PROBABLY with a STUPID SEAGULL!"

Eilra looked at Eraser as if he was going daft. "W...w...what do yar thum thar wan' me t'do? I 'aven't a clue..."

"FIND them! BEFRIEND them! LOOK after them!" cackled Eraser. "If they get the Festalpod, HELP them return it to the Juvitree!"

"Shall I pass on yar regards, so I should?" Eilra asked helpfully.

"NO, YOU BLITHERING IDIOT! THEY'RE MY ENEMIES!" Eraser looked at Shystar. "Tell him in your nice way before I lose my TEMPER!"

Shystar put a 'comforting' arm around Eilra's small shoulders. "Eraser would be very upset if you were to mention his name... you understand."

"I thum thar don't understand, so I don't but I does try!" quivered Eilra.

"You see," Shystar smiled, "he likes to keep his affairs very private... secret even. So run along and be very careful."

"Yar be thum thar careful of the suck-abogs, so you should," said Eilra, looking at Eraser holding up the prismatrans as a silent reminder.

"WHAT SUCKABOGS?" Eraser yelled.

"Thum ones tha' suck yar beneath the great lake an' into thum thar Lurkamungoo, so they do."

"WE'LL BE WAITING FOR YOU!" Eraser shouted after him.

Suckalogged

The crashed Beamsurfer lay at an awkward angle amongst the humid jungle of giant fungi. Clusters of toadstools stood as high as pine trees, their huge red caps crammed together like enormous, overcrowded umbrellas. Puffball fungi, the size of boulders, tightly hugged the mushy black soil; at the slightest touch, clouds of spores puffed into the steamy, greenish-grey atmosphere. All was deadly quiet except for the constant plopping of slime-drips echoing notes of eerie caution.

Zag and Eggbert had shakily struggled out of the Beamsurfer to assess the damage. "At least the fungi cushioned the initial impact," said Zag, not finding anything obvious. "Difficult to see what's happened the other side," he sighed, seeing how much of the rest of the craft was embedded in a

large patch of soggy ground.

"It's well sunk into that boggy bit," said Eggbert, peering at the half-submerged, frisbee-like base. "I can see we've got one heck of a problem."

"Even I know that!" squawked Flewy, beak poking out of the sloping cockpit door in time to receive a large blob of slime directly on his helmet. "YEEEEUUUK!" he shrieked, nearly shaking his head off to rid himself of the ooze-dripping indignity.

"Don't knock it pal," said Eggbert, "it may bring ya luck!"

"I NEED SOME PAPER!" Flewy screeched, as the muck drizzled down his goggles and onto his beak.

"No point pal," replied Eggbert. "If that was a bird that plopped ya, it's miles away by now!"

"That's not helpful!" Flewy shrieked, disappearing back inside the Beamsurfer.

"And neither are you, ya irritat..."

"Leave him," said Zag. "We've more urgent matters to deal with." He fumbled through his Thingummajacket and found his Cosmo-fob. "If I can contact Lucy, we may find..."

"Eggna and Awoo," said Eggbert, accidentally nudging Zag with an excited flap of his great wings and nearly making him drop it. "Oops, sorry pal."

With a juggle and a kindly grin Zag held the device in the palm of his hand and mind-activated it. To his surprise, unlike when he tried to contact William, the vista-globe burst forth like a fountain of stardust. He concentrated to increase the size of the vista-globe and so gain a better view.

"WOW that's cool!" exclaimed Eggbert. "What's happening?"

A section of a galleon's deck appeared within the sparkling haze. "It's on the *Mobsea Dick*, that's what's happening," replied Zag, seeing the totally unexpected.

Eggbert couldn't believe it either. "But we saw Lucy trying ta escape the vortex with Eggna and Awoo!"

"Either she's dropped it or she's there

somewhere!" said Zag, mind-activating and manoeuvring Lucy's Cosmo-fob to roam the deck. They gasped at the sight of the broken main mast, with fallen ropes and canvas adding to the devastation.

Eggbert was eager to get to the *Mobsea Dick* as soon as possible. "If I step into the image, will it work like the twins' painting set?" he asked, recalling their last adventure, when he and Awoo had stood by the easel, and were whisked into the painting of *Blot* and transported onto that island in a flash.

"If only," sighed Zag, looking keenly at the vista-globe. "I haven't had time to program in the qualities of the Thingummagadgetal Painting Set."

"Would that take ya long to do?"

"Unfortunately it's back at the barn... but at least the roaming program is functioning," he answered, anxious to see if anybody at all was still on board.

"This is amazing." Eggbert watched just as anxiously but he was also in awe of his friend's genius.

"It flies around like an oversized bee without a buzz," said Zag, as if it wasn't clever at all. "It's still in the testing stage, so let's hope it keeps working," he added, making Lucy's Cosmo-fob roam further. It travelled along the deck as he skilfully mind-guided it, avoiding the many fallen obstacles which lay strewn everywhere. "I'll try to get below deck," said Zag, but every hatch he managed to locate was firmly shut.

Eggbert's keen eyes monitored each stage of the remote Cosmo-fob's progress. "I'm sure I saw a hole in the deck, or it might have been a stain or something."

"Got to be worth checking out," said Zag, retracing the search.

"It's there!" said Eggbert trying hard to keep cool and not mess up the procedure. "Just a little to the right of that closed hatch and back a bit." Unbeknown to him, this was the hole made by the wrigglies, which Catpone had fallen through.

Flewy's beak reappeared over the cockpit's tilting doorway. "Now's not the time to be playing with your stupid TOYS!" he shrieked.

"Now's NOT the time for YOUR stupidity, PAL!" Eggbert replied angrily.

"HUH! I know when I'm not wanted," squawked Flewy, ducking some slime-blobs and disappearing back into the Beamsurfer.

Zag concentrated hard on taking Lucy's Cosmo-fob down into the *Mobsea Dick*, just managing to avoid the steps from the hatch. "I recognise that area; Catpone's cabin is a little further down the passageway." But the enclosed space made the Cosmo-fob difficult to control and, without any warning, it bumped into something which fortunately was very soft.

"Listen ya wimp, now's not der time tuh be womantic so stop yuh nudging or I'll put yuh in one of 'em balloon-finggies personally!"

"Legs, where are you?" Zag shouted into the vista-globe.

"Looking for muh lipstick an' about tuh thump dis dipstick."

Catpone jumped, seeing Zag's activated image. "Uh... Zag what's wiv der uh... ghosty business."

"Don't worry, Catpone, I'm an incarnation."

"Uh... uh... Legs, Zag's gone nuts, he finks he's uh... posy! Uh... tell 'im wuh need don't need flowers an' dis ain't no wedding!"

"Outta my way, stupid." Legs looked far from her normal pristine self, it was obvious she had been doing more than her bit to fight off the Lurks.

"Where are you?" asked Zag.

"On a slimy, ponging sea, twying tuh dodge dose 'owwible fwlying fings dat look like dose Gutwumble wacked bufaw he gave yuh dat memento – dar same ones dat nicked William. Duh punks keep weturning tuh bombard us wiv dem balloons. For duh pwesent dey can't get frew duh *Mobsea*'s wigging but dere's not much left."

"Have they captured any of you?" Zag asked.

"No, but Lucy, Eggna an' Awoo musta

copped it whun wuh whooshed down dat plughole."

"Where are the rest of the Mogsters?" asked Zag, keeping a brave face.

"Wiv Gutwumble hiding under canvas waiting to wack 'em whun dey twy tuh board us again. He wants tuh put 'em on der menu."

"Get the crew to criss-cross the top decks with ropes and nets," urged Zag. "Meanwhile we'll try to contact Astral and his Defend..."

"Dey're attacking us again!" As Legs shouted her image bounced around inside the vista globe.

Zag tried hard to keep in touch but without success – all contact was lost. "Let's hope the Cosmoputa's working," said Zag, rushing to scramble aboard the Beamsurfer, "we could do with Astral's help!"

Without mercy or warning, the boggy section of the gooey soil swirled and bubbled furiously. Zag and Eggbert just managed to keep clear as the craft slid rapidly into the centre of the gurgling whirlpool.

"HELP ME!" screeched Flewy. Desperately struggling to climb out, he accidentally touched the emergency central-locking button and the cockpit door slid shut, trapping him inside the craft. His pleading, helmeted face pressed hard against the window as, with a colossal slurp, the bog cruelly swallowed the Beamsurfer down through the vortex and into a miry tomb.

Zag and Eggbert were left staring in horror at Flewy's plight.

The fungi Jungle

Unaware they were being watched by a pair of anxious eyes, Zag and Eggbert stood in stunned silence, staring at the bog as if hoping that the Beamsurfer would pop up with Flewy squawking some insult.

"I feel real bad about telling the little guy off," Eggbert muttered.

"You shouldn't be troubled." Zag smiled sadly. "It was his way and, ironically, it was what was so loveable about Flewy."

"Wouldn't stand by thar furr too long." A short doddery stranger stood not far behind them, dressed in green gardening wellies and mildew-ridden, oversized oilskins, complete with a baggy hood. "Thum thar soon tha whole of Telijencia'll disappear inta one big suckabog... Yar mark me words, an' so be it furr certain."

"Did ya say Telijencia?" gasped Eggbert.

"Tha's worr I said... Thum thar suckabogs arr gitting nigh on impossible to avoid. Still, at least tha others some'ow managed it, so they did."

"You did say others?" queried Zag, peering closely at the odd looking individual.

"Tha's worr I said," replied the stranger, pulling back his hood to reveal a well-worn, glowing face. "Thum thar big eagle... slightly smaller than yur friend 'ere but more bedraggled, an owl o' sorts, an' thum thar young lady... very pretty thing so she is... they're friends o' yurs I take it kindly?"

"Much more than buddies," Eggbert sighed with relief, "and we're so pleased to meet ya."

"Likewise certainly," the stranger smiled, "me name's Marshtitch... Eilrach Marshtitch... jus' call me Eilra for short, on accounta me height."

"Do you know where they are?" asked Zag.

"Don' yar wurry yurselves, yar friends arr being amply looked arfter by me thum thar wife Nala, so they arr to tha good of all."

"We're certainly grateful to you too, Eilra. This is Eggbert and I'm Zag," he said, offering to shake Eilra's small but very grubby hand.

"Tuh be thum thar honest..." Eilra prattled, trying to quickly wipe his hand clean on his greasy oilskins, "...me wife's name's Nala Britelock," he chit-chatted, as he made his hand even dirtier. "We nevva 'ad thum chance furr a proper wedding so we married ourselves properly or improperly which evva ways yuh wish to take it..."

Zag smiled politely and, completely disregarding the slime, firmly shook Eilra's hand.

"...Anyways as far's I'm concerned she's a Marshtitch," Eilra added with a wink, glad to have his hand back. "Yu'd better follow me and make jolly sure yar thum thar tread where I doo."

"Don't mean to be personal," said Eggbert, following carefully in Eilra's welly-steps, "but ya a Rutilan, aren't ya?"

"Furr sure I'm that," smiled Eilra, "Nala and I use'tuh 'elp thum thar fellow Rutilans put thar glow in thar sunset but we liked gardening so much we volunteered to look arfter tha Juvitree, so we did."

"It's just that ya seemed to be…" Eggbert tried to put it delicately, "No offence meant, but Rutilans faces are always glowing and don't have wrinkles like you do."

"Ever since thum Lurks stole thar Festalpod, everything 'ere ends up going decrepit, an' so yar might as well know it, so yar should." Eilra carefully lead them past a swampy ditch. "'Tis more 'Fester' than Festal with what thum Lurks done 'ere," Eilra pointed to a gap through some slime-oozing rocks, "'cos fester's whar thum 'ere place be doing, so 'tis, furr sure."

With great difficulty and not much success, Eggbert was trying to keep the slime from covering his feathers. "I guess this is what happens when the Festalpod's kept out of the Juvitree?"

"Strikes me, though more in 'ope thun

certainty, yur knows more thun yur wish t'be saying, if only?" Eilra puffed, stopping to take a rest.

"If only what?" asked Zag, as he and Eggbert also took a breather.

"Jus' silly-dreaming tha one day some-one'll thum thar jus' turn up an' restore thum 'ere Telijencia back to creativity, so I wish oftimes." Eilra gazed upwards despairingly. "Anyways thar'll nevvar 'appen t'be sure 'cos they'd 'ave tuh find this 'ere place first off, an' even thar's aside from gitting thar Festalpod, somehow impossible so 'tis."

Neither Zag or Eggbert made a comment. Both wanted to see Lucy, Eggna and Awoo before they would commit themselves further.

From high above in the toadstooled canopy, a shower of slime-balls scored direct hits on the threesome. They could hear horrid, squeak-gurgling, scornful laughter as a troop of tentacle-armed membraned sacs of dripping goo splurtle-swung from toadstool to toadstool. Unlike monkeys swinging from branch to branch, these stuck to one trunk-like stem, then spurted off like water-rockets to stick to another. Some jumped into gurgling suckabogs, which looked like enormous, mildew-covered cowpats, and disappeared just like the Beamsurfer, never to be seen again.

"What the...?" Eggbert tried in vain to duck away from the onslaught.

"Globlins," said Eilra. "I shud ignore thum critters, they'll make yar lose concentration and yar'll fall in a suckabog furr certain, most definite."

The fungi jungle was far too dense for Eggbert to fly even the shortest distance, so he was forced to plod on, unable to react to the annoying Globlins covering them in slime. He and Zag followed Eilra through the maze of giant Puffballs. Clambering through the boulder-like fungi they triggered dusty cloud-puffs of spores into the steamy air, some impudently attaching themselves to the sopping, scrambling trio.

Zag's and Eggbert's eyes watered,

irritated by the greyish spores and both had taken on the guise of grimy snowmen. Zag let out one huge sneeze and managed to control another. "Uhuhuh… how much further?"

"Jus'about near shortly," said Eilra, leading them downhill, along a stepped tunnel hollowed out of the giant stalk of a fallen toadstool. Zag and Eggbert were amazed that underneath the rotting fungi existed a semi-sunken, lopsided, stone cottage.

"Now where's thum door key, lost it 'ave I no maybe," Eilra mumbled, searching his pockets.

"Sad wha's 'appened to yuh friend but least tha others are thum thar safe… furr tha time being anyways, so how they arr."

Still shocked by the loss of Flewy, Zag shook his head in grateful disbelief. "At least something good's happened."

"Ya need a door key here?" asked Eggbert.

"Be thum thar vigilant at all times," Eilra said, finding his key and pushing the distorted door, "tha's thar best advice I can give anyhow."

Nala's wizened face glowed with relief as she kissed Eilra. "More guests m'dear, ain't seen nobody furr this long-time now we're fair inundated."

"So sorry to intrude, especially in the mess we're in," Zag apologised, wiping his feet on the doormat and taking off his fez before entering.

"Jus' teasing," she smiled, "pleased I'm sure." Her squat form, bordering the rotund, was exaggerated by her green oilskin dress as she curtsied.

They followed Nala into the sloping hallway. Though in poor condition, everything was neat and tidy, but the cottage was dimmed from the outside by rotting debris which virtually blocked every window.

Awoo opened one tired eye as they entered the small lounge, couldn't believe it, so he opened the other to make sure. Perched on the back of the sofa, he looked like a sentry watching over Lucy, who lay curled up fast asleep. "Shssh," he said protectively, as Eggna made a fuss of Eggbert.

"Bless her," smiled Eggna, as Zag bent over to kiss Lucy's forehead, "she cried herself to sleep about William and all that's happened to us. Lucy grabbed Awoo and I tried to fly off the *Mobsea Dick* clutching them in my talons. But the force from the whirlpool's vortex was too strong and it sucked us here, separated from the Mogster's ship. It was then we were found in the fungi jungle and brought here by Nala."

"It's okay, ya did ya best, an no more could be asked," Eggbert comforted.

"We won't wake up Lucy yet," whispered Zag, "I'm afraid there's more bad news. We've lost Flewy and the..."

"That's about the only thing that doesn't surprise me, old chap," Awoo puffed his feathers. "He'll soon be back wanting another award for doing nothing."

"Except this time I fear he's gone for always," Zag continued sadly. "He and the Beamsurfer fell prey to a suckabog."

"Look I'm sorry... I didn't mean to..." Awoo stumbled over his words, feeling guilty about his untimely comment.

"Horrible end for the little guy," sighed Eggbert, "to be trapped inside."

"If the Mogsters are gone too," Eggna remarked, "we're the only ones left."

"*If* is a small word with a big meaning," Zag frowned thoughtfully.

"Thum thar strikes me thar ain't much yar can doo," said Eilra, passing a basket of fungi to Nala, "especially if they've bin thum thar globollised, more than certain maybe."

"In thum big Globolloony things," Nala added, nervously grasping handfuls of fungi and squeezing the juices into a large earthenware jug.

"That's what happened to William!" said Lucy, startling everybody by sitting bolt upright.

"Now ya rest easy," consoled Eggna.

"I'm okay." Lucy smiled and went to give Zag a cuddle. "I've been listening and telling myself to be brave and now I am."

"That's great, little lady," Eggbert smiled, "but ya must understand..."

Lucy interrupted, "I dreamt William told me not to lie about moping. When Zag said the word *if* has a big meaning I realised we can't be sure about anything unless we try."

"Exactly." Zag gave Lucy a hug. "And what's more you're very special and precious, so between us all who knows what's possible."

"Now listen m'dears, before yar all do summut foolish," Nala wiped her hands on a grubby cloth. "Thum Lurks'll 'ave yar as soon as look at yar, an' yur'd be putricity for thur slithersticks in no time a'all."

"Putricity?" Awoo shuddered.

"Tha's right, it's fuel ta make thum fly. They store yar in Globolloons first, thur like huge snotty balloons, thun yar..." Nala trembled at the memory of her narrow escape as she left the murky liquid to settle.

"Did you say 'store'?" queried Zag.

"Thars wha' she said," replied Eilra, "thun yar put in thum thar wobbling big Putrisphere whur yar energy's sapped, yar life's dimmed, an' yur in Globscurity, a horrible place where yar don't matter any more, an' tha's essactly it."

"Stored where?" asked Zag, keen to pursue any glimmer of hope.

"In thum thar Lurkamungoo," replied Eilra, "below thum thar great lake, now stagnant an' all smelly 'orrible."

"Deary me, furgot thum cups an' tharr," said Nala, leaving the room, "but don' yar worry m'dears, the Defenders told Eilra to look arfter yar."

"What Defenders?" asked Zag, but Nala had left the room.

"I'll jus' be back's a whiff." Eilra suddenly rushed after her." I... I need tuh 'elp me Nala in thum thar kitchen... so I do quickly."

Twists of fate

With his beak tucked into his rear, Flewy was far too frightened to find out what was constantly banging on the cockpit door. The probability of Zag or anybody else coming to rescue him had ranged from possibly-maybe to highly unlikely.

"WHY ME?" squeaked Flewy, facing the stark reality that if he stayed inside the Beamsurfer he would most likely die of fear. He was so confused, he'd even thought he'd heard William's voice. More out of curiosity than courage, he peeked through the cockpit window to see something fuzzy-rippling outside.

"Is anybody in there?" called a faint voice, as the door was thumped again.

"HELP, IT'S A GHOST!" shrieked Flewy, his Antiwobble-finthruster preventing all his feathers from standing on end.

"Let me in quickly!" said William. "It's me and I'm not a ghost!"

"GO AWAY AND HAUNT SOME-ONE ELSE!" Flewy squawked.

"Even if I were a ghost, I'd be friendly!" William shouted.

Flewy pressed the button and opened the cockpit door. "WIPE YOUR FEET!" he screeched, trying to make out William's spectre-like figure as he climbed aboard, dripping slime, "if you've still got any!"

"Close it," said William, reverting back to normal. "And make sure it's locked," he added, as he accidentally shoved passed Flewy in his rush to press a button on the cockpit's control panel.

"A 'please' or 'thank you' would be nice!" Flewy huffed indignantly. "Anyway, how did you do that?"

"I'll tell you later," answered William, finding the correct button on the dashboard and making sure the Beamsurfer was now Chameleonised. "I was hoping Zag would be in here."

"Charming!" squawked Flewy, taking William's comment as a direct insult. "It's a wonder you even bothered to find me by accident!" His remark prompted curiosity. "How did you find me anyway?"

"I didn't mean it like that and you know it," said William. "I heard a big slurping and gurgling sound and followed it to see what was happening, thinking it might be a way out." William tried to start up the Cosmoputa but without success.

"Yet another of Zag's gadgets, well past its sell-by date," quipped Flewy rudely.

"Then why are you wearing one?" replied William, pointing at Flewy's Antiwobble-finthruster outfit. He tried again to make the Cosmoputa work.

"I hope you're not fiddling with something you know nothing about!" said Flewy. "On the other hand maybe I can make it work," he added perching on the control panel, "I'm good at fiddling with things."

"DON'T!" said William, pushing him aside. "If I can't make it work, we'll have to stay here and try to come up with a plan. In the meantime, let's hope and pray Zag finds us before..."

"Huh! I know when I'm not appreciated!" Flewy squawked, huffily slapping the control panel repeatedly with his foot. "Anyway he's probably forgotten all about me and is with that grump Eggbert looking for those stupid Mogsters."

Trapped on the lake and aboard the battered *Mobsea Dick*, the Mogster crew were undergoing a brief respite from the continuous pounding by the Lurks. All the masts had been felled by the Globolloons but the crew had managed to outwit them by following Zag's advice and stringing ropes across the top decks.

Mindful of his responsibilities, Gutrumble took the opportunity to mess about in the galley, experimenting with the menu for Zag's award dinner. Confident in his ability to knock anybody scatty, he was certain the Lurks had been licked. Unbeknown to him, his confidence took a more literal sense as he sucked on one of the many Festalmaggots he had stored in demijohns, the large bottles with a short narrow necks normally used for making wine. "Dese wrigglies taste SOH good!" he exclaimed all chef-like, patting the portable supply he'd put in smaller jars tied to his belt, which chinked around his gross belly as a reminder of his good fortune.

Suddenly the fur on the back of his thick neck stood on end; he sensed something weird was slithering up behind him. With reflexes that belied his fat gut, he spun around, lunging out a huge, grotty paw and accidentally smashing the stack of thick glass demijohns he'd filled with writhing Festalmaggots. With an almighty thud, Malodour fell motionless in an oozing pool of slime. Gutrumble hauled him up in one clawed paw, picking up his chef's hat and the slitherstick in the other.

Catpone rushed down the ladderway to see what had happened. "Uh... Guts... uh who's yah... what's duh...?" he yelled.

"It's a biggun, Boss." Gutrumble proudly held up the Lurk for Catpone to see, then sniffed at it.

"Uh... put it on da menu... Guts," Catpone inspected it closely, "it looks uh... testy."

"Tasty, Boss," corrected Gutrumble. "Testy's when yuh iwwitable."

"Uh... it's gonna be vewy annoyed if it... uh... wakes up, Guts."

"Dis won't cos it's gone permanent bye-byes, Boss."

Catpone touched the limp, oozy skin. "Uh... I have a digestion."

"I fink ya mean suggestion, Boss," burped Gutrumble.

"Uh... yeah. Uh... we could keep it fuh Zag's award dinner and smuvver it in uh... cloister sauce."

"Good idea, Boss. But I fink ya mean oyster sauce."

"CATPONE, COME 'ERE YAH WIMP! DUH MOBSEA'S SINKING!" Legs roared towards the galley.

"Don't be uh... stupid Legs, da *Mobsea* can't do no finking."

"I'm f...finking," burped Gutrumble, "dat Legs said *sinking*, Boss!"

Catpone and Gutrumble rushed to look down into the very hold which had once imprisoned the twins and Awoo. The escaped Festalmaggots had eaten holes which made the hull timbers look like a colander.

"I'm sinking wuh finking," said Catpone, taking an unwanted shower.

Restless

Zag waited for Eilra and Nala to return from their kitchen to answer his question. Being a guest, he hadn't wished to appear rude by following them.

The Rutilans brought in the cups and spread them on the rickety table propped with books to compensate for the sloping floor.

"You mentioned Defenders?" said Zag, trying to pursue the matter amid the bustle and fuss of them pouring the murky spore-broth into the cups.

Nala briefly clasped each full cup in her hands, bringing it nearly to the boil. "Purrfickt, warms tha very soul," she smiled, carefully passing one to Lucy. "Not all fungi's poisonous m'dear but yar need tuh know wha' to look furr."

"Rarrthar dim in 'ere," said Eilra, ferreting some knobbly stubby brown candles from a draw. "Tuh think we looked over tha sunlit lake once, so we did." Flicking his thumb and forefinger he produced a flame. "Thum past glow-into-sunset skills arr still useful," he reminisced.

"Please don't waste them," Zag urged. "We really need to discuss how to find our friends."

"And ya must be short on wax." Eggbert added to Zag's request.

"No problem, we get it from our ears." Nala offered the murky looking spore-broth, "We've constant supplies."

"If you don't mind I'll pass on the broth," said Awoo, trying to disguise a grimace and remain polite at the same time.

"What Defenders did you see?" asked Zag. Fully concentrating on his need for an answer, he forgot the cottage floor sloped badly, placed his cup on it, spilt half of his broth and tried to wipe it up.

"It's all right, m'dear," chuckled Nala, "it

'appens all the time."

"Thank you," Zag smiled apologetically. "Tell me, did you see Astral?"

"Astral?" slurped Eilra.

"You should know him, he's the leader of the Defenders," said Lucy, wondering why he appeared not to recognise the name.

Eilra stopped sipping his spore-broth. "Me golly-gosh did yar hear that Nala, thum thar Astral's been promoted, so he has, it sounds like?"

"Always thought 'im t'be nice, not least very 'andsome," she replied, "I'm glad he has an' no doubt he thum thar deserves it."

Eilra gave her a knowing glance. "Larst we heard, thum thar wretched Eraser was in charge, so he was."

"An' I'm wondering wha'appened?" sighed Nala.

"That's another story," Zag interrupted with an air of frustration. "We value your hospitality but we must find the Defenders," he said firmly.

"Tha be very risky," Eilra shook his head.

"Best stay put. Telijencia's not warr it was an' thar's many hidden dangers lurking to get you, so 'tis."

"Then maybe ya can help us find them?" suggested Eggbert.

"Trouble is thur Vernal Eclipse is nigh upon us." Nala offered more spore-broth but received polite refusals. "Thar fungi jungle'll be full o'thum Globlins ready to trap yar in suckabogs. Thay'll be ajumping ins an' out o'thum 'sif thurs no tomorrows."

"Eggbert and I can find the Defenders and bring them here," said Eggna.

"Not a good idea with thum thar Lurks flying 'bout, no 'tis," said Eilra. "Thar lake's nigh as big as an ocean, it jus' gets bigger all thar time."

Nala looked despondent. "It's so vast, the whole place's sinking into Lurkamungoo, including this 'ere dear little cottage."

"All the more reason to do something about it," said Lucy bravely.

"If everything's sinking," sighed Awoo, "it'll be us next!"

"That's clever thinking, Awoo!" Zag complimented, "Eilra said Lurkamungoo was below the lake and that must be how we get into it."

"It was a statement not an idea," Awoo pontificated. "I know things are desperate but I think we can do without crazy suggestions."

Zag's Thingummajacket began to buzz; he reached into it and pulled out his Cosmo-fob. To their astonishment, the vista-globe burst into life and William's face appeared together with Flewy's.

"Hey Zag it's me!" said William, "I'm in the Beamsurfer."

Lucy's eyes flooded with happy tears and she was momentarily lost for words.

"And me!" squawked Flewy.

"IT'S SO GOOD TO SEE YOU," chuckled Zag, mighty pleased to see them. The others kept quiet as he spoke to William. "What's it like down there?" he asked.

"Slimy and horrible," William explained.

"It's a huge cavernous-type place with lots of gooey tunnels and where everything's spongy and..."

"It's like being in Gutrumble's stomach," squawked Flewy, "it stinks down here!"

"I managed to Chameleonise the Beamsurfer," said William.

"Well done," Zag smiled. "Is the Festalpod still there?"

William searched and found it in the cockpit compartment. "Yes," he said, showing it to them. Eilra and Nala huddled together agog at the sight of the Festalpod.

"Stay where you are, we will be with you very soon," Zag grinned.

"Tell Lucy she's the bestest sister in the world," said William.

"Luv you too," shouted Lucy.

"Wish someone loved me," squawked Flewy.

"We all do," said Zag, "don't we Awoo?"

"Don't be long," said Flewy, cheekily blowing Awoo a kiss, "I know how easily you get side-tracked."

"Ahem," Awoo coughed, as the images disappeared. "LOVE! That's a bit of a strong word. I'm an owl, not a peacock, old chap."

"So how do we get to William and Flewy?" asked Lucy.

"Interesting question," Zag smiled, "because I reckon the suckabog the Beamsurfer sank into leads to Lurkamungoo and directly to William and Flewy. They can't be far from the surface because we received a clear signal."

"Thum Lurks caught Nala once then released her up a suckabog," commented Eilra. "We nevvar thought of jumping back into one or wished to for tha matter, so be it for certain."

"Very wise, old chap, considering all the circumstances," said Awoo, authoritatively.

"Eilra and Nala, we need your help immediately," Zag urged. "Can you take us back to the suckabog where the Beamsurfer sank?"

"I 'ears what yar saying so be it I wish otherwise," said Eilra. "We'll take yar. Thun

I'll try and find the Defenders, tell thum what's 'appened an' that yar need help, so I will."

"Eggna and I can fly out through the gap in the toadstools made by the Beamsurfer when we crashed," suggested Eggbert. "We'll search the Lake for the *Mobsea Dick*."

"An' Nala can wait for yar return up thar suckabog and she'll show yar where thar Juvitree is." Eirla hurried Nala to put on her oilskin jacket. "I'll meet yar all there to replace the Festalpod, Lurks permitting."

"We're grateful to ya both, pal," smiled Eggbert.

"Just one thing bothers me," said Awoo. "How do we go down through the bog?"

Zag tapped his Thingummajacket. "By umbrella," he grinned.

"By UMBRELLA?" Awoo gasped.

"Trust me," Zag chuckled.

Down the Plughole

Eilra and Nala led the strenuous hike through the dense Fungi Jungle, their pace slowed by Eggna and Eggbert who were cumbersome under such conditions. Lucy kept close to Zag, and Awoo was perched on his shoulder, flapping his wings to maintain balance at each stumble. The whole place was restless, filled with the piercing noise of hyperactive Globlins.

Everything around them was undergoing rapid change – certainly not for the better. The once greenish-grey humidity was fast becoming a pure misty green heralding Telijencia's fruitless effort to rejuvenate. Clusters of massive toadstools bent precariously as their tree-trunk stems turned patchy-black like over-ripe bananas. Heavy, pulpous chunks crashed down from huge caps, breaking apart as they smashed against each other prior to their ultimate downfall.

"I thum thar warned yar 'bout it, so I did kindly," said Eilra, dodging some debris as he stopped to take his bearings amongst the wilting fungi. "We've t'be quicker else it be difficult t'find thum thar suckabog, 'fore it gets too confusing, so 'tis," he said, as new clusters of toadstools sprung forth rapidly to replace the fallen and change the festering landscape.

"LOOK OUT!" Zag shouted, jolting Awoo off his perch by grabbing Nala in the nick of time from the path of a falling stem-trunk. Awoo panicked, fluttered the wrong way and was hit a glancing blow from the crashing toadstool. A huge puffball fungi, squashed by the weighty load, gasped out its innards to the fallen giant fungi. Awoo lay trapped somewhere underneath the rotten debris.

Coughing and spluttering from the effects of spore-dust, Zag took a bowie-knife from his Thingummajacket. His eyes streamed with the irritation, as he vigorously sliced at the fungi to rescue his friend. Eggbert and Eggna pounced onto the stem-trunk, tearing away lumps with their beaks and talons. Holding a handkerchief over her nose and mouth, Lucy crouched down seeking signs of life – Awoo was nowhere to be seen.

Globlins spurted from trunk to trunk screech-cackling, as if laughing at the predicament below. Accurately aimed slime-balls rained down from the snotty-green creatures intent on distracting and luring the rescuers to their doom. Furious at being ignored, their screeches became scream-piercing insults, higher pitched and more shattering to the ear.

"Tis ain't too good, so 'tis not," complained Eilra, as he and Nala took cover the best they could against a slimy, spongy rock.

The ground began to gurgle, dislodging the stem-trunk from its resting place and allowing Awoo to poke his beak through a gap in the rotting fungi. But the sticky soil had him stuck in its tacky grip.

"There he is!" shouted Lucy.

As she reached in and grabbed hold of Awoo, the gurgling became a sudden whirlpool and she was dragged into its murk, yelling for help. With no room to fly, the eagles were left helpless to stop Lucy and Awoo being whirled towards the centre.

Zag leapt onto the broken stem-trunk and just managed to retain his balance. As it spun slowly in the momentum he reached inside his Thingummajacket and took out his Thingummagadgetal Umbrella. "GRAB THIS!" he called out, expanding its shaft to twice the length of a walking-stick. Lying flat on the trunk, Zag offered the handle but Lucy's grasp missed it.

Although it took no time at all, it seemed an age as he waited for the swirling momentum to yield another opportunity. The vortex was beginning to form at the centre, its cruel mouth fast growing into a suck-gaping plughole. Zag knew his next chance could be the last. Lucy's arm remained outstretched as Awoo, too sodden to fly, clung to her clothes. Offering the handle once more, Zag nearly lost his grip on the stem-trunk but this time he was successful. Ironically, the swirling motion helped his effort to pull them alongside.

As if in a final attempt to distract, the Globlins dive-bombed and disappeared into the ever-expanding suckabog. Nearby, a whole cluster of giant Toadstools collapsed and crashed to the ground, momentarily adding to the danger, but then creating an opportunity. Left with just enough room to fly, Eggbert and Eggna went to Zag's assistance but time was running out fast.

"Awoo, climb onto Lucy's shoulder," Zag instructed. "Lucy, step onto the handle as I feed the shaft through your hands. Eggna, keep us steady and Eggbert, help me haul them up."

Eggna gripped the stem-trunk with her talons and spread her wings, flapping gently to stop it from rolling over as Lucy and Awoo were pulled aboard beside Zag on the ever-disintegrating fungi 'life-raft'.

Zag had caught sight of the temporary gaps in the jungle's canopy. "Go quickly, we'll be okay!" he urged the eagles. "That's your chance... find the *Mobsea Dick*!"

"They can't leave us stranded!" hooted Awoo, nearly deafening Lucy's ear as Eggna and Eggbert took off into the darkened, green sky.

"Stranded? Not us!" said Zag, with Lucy clinging to him as he held up the umbrella and pressed a button on its shaft to extend it another two metres. "We're off down to Lurkamungoo."

"What about returning the FESTAL-POD?" shouted Eilra. "Thar's not thum thar right suckabog, methinks not... Or could be, I don't know!"

The umbrella's canopy opened like an enormous inverted tulip spreading its petals wide. Rotating gently, it helped Zag keep their balance as he flicked a catch and released a collapsible seat into which he helped Lucy. Somewhat reluctantly, but with no choice, Awoo still remained perched on her shoulder.

Zag shouted to Eilra, "Go tell the Defenders!" Zag just managed to gain a foothold on the umbrella's handle before the stem-trunk completely broke apart. For a few moments the rotating 'petals' kept them hovering above the swirling suckabog.

"I hope what ever you're doing works!" Awoo said, scared out of his twits – unlike Lucy who had every confidence in Zagwitz.

"It's my Brellycopter," said Zag, with all the confidence in the world, and reached for another button. "Like an umbrella, it goes up when it's down and down when it's up. We're up and going down so HOLD ON TIGHT!" He pressed the button, the canopy shut around them like a cocoon and they whooshed down into the suckabog like a rocket going the wrong way.

Zag, Lucy and Awoo heaved with disgust as they travelled down the vortex of the suckabog and into Lurkamungoo – an experience they would never forget. It was like

slithering through an enormous, bog-drip-
ping, mucus-lined plughole then being post-
ed through a greasy flap to land on a sopping
mass of warm, raw liver.

Lucy and Awoo stood patiently as Zag
retracted his Brellycopter to pocket-size. Its
gunky state was so bad that, instead of putting it back inside his Thingummajacket, Zag
hid it in a sinewy crevice he'd spotted in the
membranous wall.

Suddenly, Globlins by the hundreds burst
from the plop-gurgling roof, forcing them to
crouch down to avoid the obnoxious surge.
Attracted by a task much more cruelly enter-
taining, the screech-cackling Globlins shot
past the threesome and onwards through the
ooze-pumping, artery-like tunnel. Their
repulsive translucent sac-bagged bodies rippled excited glows of yellow and green, giving a temporary but better light to the murk-
iness.

"There it is!" Lucy exclaimed, more
excited at the prospect of being reunited
with her twin brother than worried about

her surroundings.

"Not so fast!" hooted Awoo, as some straggler Globlins whooshed past his head. Still perched safely on her shoulder, he'd no wish to land on the gooey floor.

"Rather defeats the whole object," muttered Zag, leading the way towards the Beamsurfer. Although Chamleonised, it stood prominently in its covering of slime. "Must find a solution to that," he added as he banged on the cockpit door.

The Molsea's Last Stand

Eraser's patience had worn so thin that if it stood sideways you wouldn't see it. Nothing dramatic had happened near the Juvitree and even he was wondering if he had overestimated the Lurks.

"Stay low!" whispered Shystar, interrupting Eraser's fruitless nostril excavation. "Look, someone's coming!"

"It's those Rutilan idiots!" barked Eraser, completely destocked of bogeys and glad to have something else to pick on. "Thought I TOLD you to look after your GUESTS!" he ranted at Nala.

"T...they've gone, so they 'ave an' I try to stop thum so I did," quaked Nala.

"GONE WHERE?" Eraser bawled.

Eilra made a feeble attempt to support his wife. "A...an' they wouldn't thum thar listen, so they didn't."

"WHO'S TALKING TO YOU?" Eraser wiped his still snotty finger on Eilra's oil-skins. Finding more muck attached to the Rutilan than was on his finger, he flicked the residue in Eilra's face.

Eilra had no option but to humbly ignore such an insult. "B...but I found thum thar white-bearded fella but he was with another eagle..."

"Take cover!" shout-whispered Shystar.

"Thur up there, so they arr," said Nala, pointing at two large flying creatures circling over the rancid lake.

"I can see that!" barked Eraser, quickly yanking Eilra and Nala to the ground. "LISTEN you pair of SHRINKHEADS, you'd better tell me what's going on!"

Eggbert and Eggna were too busy scanning the lake for the *Mobsea Dick* to notice any-thing happening on the shoreline. They soared high into the sky and spotted a mass of blackness darting around in the green haze.

Swooping ever closer, they clearly saw the Lurkwarriors circling around like vultures over helpless prey and realised the Mogsters' galleon was in dire straits. Not being able to fly into the mass, they decided to attack the stragglers and work their way in towards the ship.

The eagles' manoeuvrability was a sight of wonder and their accuracy deadly. Intercepting the Lurkwarriors one by one, they hit them with full force, sinking their lethal talons into blubbery flesh. Each time their grotesque foe would wriggle and writhe helplessly as its slitherstick spiralled down into the lake like a lost javelin. When hanging limp and lifeless, each was released to fall into the same watery grave.

Catpone was standing knee-deep in water on the top deck as a couple of slithersticks just missed him. "Hey... uh... Guts, who's chucking dere uh... piles?"

"Poles, Boss!" corrected Gutrumble, who had decided that things were tougher than expected and was trying to undo his rusted violin case to get at his trusty cutlass.

"Hey... Uh, Guts!" shouted Catpone, as some black lumps of blubber splashed down beside him, "it's waining uh... Burps!"

"Lurps, Boss," said Guts, tempted to forget his cutlass and save them for the freezer.

The *Mobsea Dick* started to pitch at the stern as if finally admitting to its lifelong lack of seaworthiness.

"MAN THE LIFEBOATS, SPOOKY!" yelled Legs.

"NEVVA HAD NONE!" Spooky replied.

The Mogster crew, though gallant in its fight to the last cat-pirate, was being left with the problem of nothing to stand on.

"ABANDON SHOP!" yelled Catpone.

"SHIP YUH BERK!" shouted Legs. "No wunda we nevva 'ad lifeboats!"

"UH... I... LEAVE YUH LEGS!"

"PLEASE YUSELF!" she yelled, jumping over the side.

"Love, Boss," corrected Gutrumble, about

to follow her, "leave is when yuh wants no one no more."

"BUT I DOOOO!" shouted Catpone, clutching Gutrumble's grotty paw as they held on their trilbies and jumped into the murky lake together.

Gutrumble floated like his own cat-made island, as the others floundered around him in the water. The Mogsters had become easy pickings for the Lurkwarriors. Globolloons burst out of their slithersticks and began to envelop the helpless crew one by one and sometimes two at a time.

Catpone surfaced to see Legs thrashing in the water, struggling to avoid drowning. He swam to her aid, stopped her from going under and held her tightly. Pained with exhaustion, she stared as if for the last time at her eye-patched hero's disfigured face. Even this deep, jagged scar which had long-time split his nose and permanently deformed his features, could not hide Catpone's concerned expression.

"Uh... dis ain't looking good, Legsy,"

he whispered.

"Yuh nevva did," she replied softly.

Spooky pointed to a Globolloon skimming towards them. "DUCK DOWN!" he yelled.

"Dat's an eagle, stupid!" Catpone replied, as he glanced the wrong way and was horrified to see first Eggbert then Eggna swallowed inside enormous Globolloons. It was a swift defeat as the murky lake finally surrendered him and every remaining Mogster to suffer the same fate – globollised!

No trace was left of the *Mobsea Dick* or its crew. All that remained were three lone trilby hats floating as escort to some items from a dainty cosmetics bag.

The Great Challenge

Having coped with Flewy's interruptions and informed Zag of the little he knew about Lurkamungoo, William explained his recent experiences to Lucy and Awoo...

"I thought I was going to die in that suck-abog," said Awoo. "It's like rancid treacle mixed with oil-spillage."

"So is a Globolloon slimy inside?" asked Lucy.

"No, it's sort of tacky but pongs like a sewer. You feel as if you can't breathe... that you have to jump around... that you must stay awake... everything outside's blurry... and when it flies through the air you feel horribly seasick... you feel as if you're going to die!"

"Looks like we soon will!" squawked Flewy, impatiently watching Zag's frustrated efforts to first operate the Cosmoputa then start up the Beamsurfer. "All that fiddling's getting us nowhere," he squawked impudently. "It's a complete waste of time so admit it, now we're all stuck!"

Zag sighed. The Beamsurfer's mechanism was well and truly gummed up with goo and the Cosmoputa was unable to send or receive signals. "Bad news, folks." Not fussed about the Festalpod's slimy condition, he picked it up and put it inside his Thingummajacket. "We can't contact Astral or the Defenders."

"Huh!" flapped Flewy, " SEE! If only you all listened to me..."

"The fact is we do," remarked Awoo, "and it gives us all a headache."

"We also can't stay here," Zag intervened, anticipating a squabble.

"Well that really does solve our problem!" squawked Flewy. "Why I'm wearing this stupid outfit I don't know! Every superhero flies around freely... and ME... NO CHANCE! All I get is blobs of slime plopped on my head, sucked down a bog into a cesspit AND then get told to..."

"Shut up?" said Lucy, raising an eyebrow.

"SEE! SEE!" shrieked Flewy.

"I was only asking," Lucy smiled.

"And I'm telling," Awoo hooted, "SHUT UP!"

A strange greenish luminosity began to penetrate the murk. Gradually becoming brighter, its rays crept towards the Beamsurfer and shone through the cockpit window.

"It's coming from the direction of the Lurks' cavern," said William. "That's where I escaped from – I saw the Lurks fly out on their slithersticks."

"That's where we must go." Without further ado Zag opened the door. "It could be our only chance to get out of here and put the Festalpod back in the Juvitree."

"Glad someone's seen the light!" quipped Flewy. "And I'm getting out first!" He set his Antiwobble-finthruster into action and hovered outside.

"Stay close together," Zag instructed, going ahead of them. "And Flewy, don't do anything stupid!"

"That's asking the impossible," muttered Awoo, perching on William's shoulder.

"I mean it," said Zag firmly.

"I heard," said Flewy, hovering.

Hardly a word was uttered as they concentrated on not slipping on the precariously slimy passage floor. The closer they crept towards the cavern with the conical roof, the louder and more frenzied the screeching and other slurp-sucking noises became. None of them were expecting what they were about to witness.

Cautiously entering the huge goo-ridden cavern, they crouched in horror. The conical roof was crammed full of Globolloons and the whole place bubbled furiously, like a plague of huge festering boils. Horrid squeak-gurgling Globlins splurted like droves of snotty-green jelly from the pulsating walls, clinging to the Globolloons and relentlessly tormenting the occupants with their boney-sticks. The more they poked and prodded, the more luminous green the cluster glowed.

Fortunately the Lurkwarriors and Globlins were far too preoccupied with their prey to spot the intruders. William noticed the mound of spongy slime that completely concealed Eraser's wrecked Cameracraft and behind which he'd previously taken cover. The mound of slime had increased even more in size, making it even more suitable to hide behind.

"We won't be seen there," he whispered.

"Let's go while they're busy." Zag grabbed hold of an indignant Flewy in case he did something stupid, and they all quickly hid behind the mound.

Zag and the others watched as one of the Globolloons, larger than the rest, proved to be a great source of frustration to the Lurkwarriors. As much as they tried to float it up to the cluster, it kept coming back down. Glowing much brighter than the others, it distended violently with the fury of its captive's pounding. The cling-film-like pair of claws protruded, dragging and tugging along the insides but to no effect.

Gudorphal blubber-wobbled impatiently. "I hope yooze lot are dealing with the last of the cat-pirates!" he spittled, anxious to get on with the more urgent task of getting hold of the Festalpod and dipping it in the Juvitree.

"That's the lot," Putridia splurt-chuckled, overjoyed at the prospect of so much putricity, "so I'll prepare the Putrisphere."

"Batch them but DON'T putrify them until Malodour's returned," Gudorphal ordered, "AND GET THAT GLOBOL-LOON UP IN THAT CLUSTER!"

Zag whispered to Lucy, William, Flewy and Awoo as they watched the Lurkwarriors link their tentacles to form a long putrid chain.

"Wait here and keep still, all of you." He took out his Cosmo-fob, chameleonised himself and crept out of hiding towards a nearby pile of discarded slithersticks, stacked more like kindling firewood than anything of importance. Zag carefully took two, making sure the pile didn't collapse and so draw attention to himself.

"Why he doesn't let me, Flewy the Supergull, scare them off, I don't know," Flewy said, flicking his beak with his wing.

"Go on then, Superdull," Awoo mocked, "and don't forget to say 'boo'. That should really scare them!"

"Shush," Lucy scolded, "don't encourage his stupidity."

"Charming," Flewy huffed, "I was only trying to be hel…"

Returning behind the mound Zag came out of chameleon guise. "William's seen the way the Lurks get out of here." He handed a slitherstick each to the twins. "I think these are mind or balance driven."

"We'll soon find out," smiled William nervously.

"Probably a bit like riding a bicycle," added Lucy.

Flewy tugged at his helmet. "What's the point in me riding on that when I'm wearing this?" he complained, tapping his outfit.

"Do as you're told," Awoo scolded,

"we've no time for your silly behaviour!"

Zag gave Lucy his Cosmo-fob, because hers was still lost. "Use this to chameleonise yourself and Awoo, that's if tucks he himself close to you."

"I'll do the same for me and Flewy," said William, taking his Cosmo-fob out of his pocket. "And mind that fin of yours," he said to Flewy.

Zag reached inside his Thingummajacket and handed William the Festalpod. "Find the Defenders and Eilra and Nala, they'll ensure this is inserted correctly in the Juvitree."

"Huh, that'll be like looking for a needle in a haystack!" quipped Flewy unhelpfully.

"Then use the speed of your Antiwobble-finthruster to find it quickly and prove you're a Supergull," Zag replied.

"But what about you?" asked Lucy anxiously.

"I'll be okay." Zag hid his uncertainty. "It's the only way. I must stop this carnage before it's too late."

"We'll try going through that vent up there," said William. "That's the vent I saw the Lurks fly through when I escaped from them."

The twins sat astride their slithersticks, Flewy and Awoo sat tucked in closely to their respective 'pilots'. With a distinct air of apprehension and lots of courage, the slithersticks were pointed upwards to the vent.

"Now go, all of you! Be brave, think clearly and be positive at all times," Zag urged, "then you'll succeed and all will be well."

"You go first, so we don't crash," said Lucy to William.

He tried but nothing happened.

"Try mind-activating it," said Zag.

Suddenly William and Flewy whooshed away, quickly followed by Lucy and Awoo. All that could be seen as they took off was a rippling gap in the middle of both slithersticks. The Cosmo-fobs had done their job chameleonising the twins and their feathery passengers, helping them to escape attention.

Zag wished them every ounce of luck as he watched them whoosh through the ooze-dripping vent high up in the cavern's wall.

Knowing that, at worst, he had to disrupt the Lurks and, at best, to stop them completely, he set about his task by taking off his fez and putting it inside his Thingummajacket. Having given his Cosmo-fob to Lucy, he pulled out a box of safety-pins and an Invisibilising Sheet of the type he had once used to hide the Beamsurfer. He had thought it redundant but his present situation proved this was not the case – although the problem remained that if dropped it was almost impossible to find.

Carefully draping the sheet over himself like a large droopy-hooded cloak, he fastened it under his chin with a safety pin. He peeped over the mound to see what was happening and saw a cluster of writhing Globolloons about to be hauled into an adjoining cavern by a gruesome chain of sucker-linked Lurkwarriors.

Wrapped in his Invisiblising Sheet, he

decided to first of all disable and immobilise the pile of discarded slithersticks and prevent them from flying or firing Globolloons. Zag delved into his Thingummajacket for a ball of Self-tangling Thingummagadgetal Componetty. Derived from the unique characteristics of a spider's web, he'd invented this for the purpose of binding leaves together for compost to prevent them from blowing around gardens. By placing two of these balls of fine thread in amongst the pile, he made sure that all the slithersticks were bound together. It would take weeks to disentangle them.

Zag followed the Lurkwarriors into the adjoining cavern which housed the Putrisphere. He felt sick at the sight of this gastric, stomach-gurgling expanse. The goo-pumping walls oozed a vile backdrop of splurting bursts of obnoxious yellow fluid as the Putrisphere throbbed its huge, inflamed, eyeball-like network of glowing red veins. Globlins darted in and out of its palpitating vent as if teasing it into a frenzy in preparation for swallowing its victims and sapping them of all their energy.

Putridia wobbled, gleefully slurp-cackling, next to Gudorphal. They were beside the hideous Putrisphere, waiting to send the Mogsters and the eagles to Globscurity.

Zag moved niftily out of the path of another chain of Lurkwarriors who were sucker-tugging the obstinate, extra-large Globolloon. They stopped beside him, exhausted. The sets of pounding claws were still at it and Zag was sure, then not so sure, that he'd heard the sound of smashing glass.

Putridia slithered alongside Gudorphal to inspect the rogue Globolloon. "Looks like we is just about ready," she slobbered.

The pounding stopped, to be replaced by a tremendous burp as the captive seemed to be scrambling on all fours inside the Globolloon, searching for something.

"What's in there?" Gudorphal splurted, "AND where's Malodour?"

"Last time I sees him he was sneaking

aboard the cat-pirates' ship to find the Festalpod?" replied Putridia.

Suddenly the Globolloon popped. Gutrumble sprang out, flattening Putridia and Gudorphal with two powerful swipes. Dazed, their flabby tentacular arms unfolded grotesquely from their blubbery torsos. The thinner third arms waved mindlessly in the centre of their foreheads. "If yuh talking about who I fink yuh are den dat's duh last yuh'll see of dat punk!" he growled, tying their arms into greasy knots.

"Hi Guts," Zag grinned broadly with astonishment and pulled back his hood. "Nice to see you."

"Hey Zag, you too," Gutrumble smiled, fumbling at his belt to suck a wriggly. But the small jars had smashed during his efforts to escape, and they had all gone. "Dem fings ate duh balloony fing," he burped, checking his backside in case that had been eaten also. "Nope, all there." He suddenly realised he could only see Zag's bearded face. "Hey pal, did dem wrigglies eat yuh body?"

"I think we should concentrate on that lot," said Zag, pointing at their attackers.

Unable to use their slithersticks, the Lurkwarriors had became frenzied and quickly formed a sucker chain surrounding Zag and Gutrumble. More and more piled in, turning the mass into a writhing wall, slowly closing in on them as if intent on suffocating them.

"MMMfffssh... mmphsh," splurtle-mumbled Gudorphal, wondering how his sink-plunger lips had got knotted in his blubbery arms.

"SHURRUP!" said Gutrumble, giving him a kick, "I'm twying tuh fink, yuh overgwown slug!"

"Mmphffsh," replied Gudorphal, in some pain.

"Slug?" said Zag quickly reaching inside his Thingummajacket. "Now that is an idea!"

Oh Slithersticks!

Lucy and William had taken to flying like Lurks take to slime. If the situation hadn't been so desperate, the whole experience would have been great fun. But they had been given a task of vital importance and had set about it with the right attitude.

The great lake was much bigger than they had imagined but, having listened to Zag's advice, neither of the twins allowed themselves to become disheartened. Beneath them the landscape was ever changing, confused by its attempts to revert back to normal. Giant toadstools grew like wildfire, only to crash down like felled trees, filling the air with spore-dust. At times it was difficult for Lucy and William to see the shores.

"Should have left some kind of marker," remarked William. "It's not going to be easy finding our way back to Zag."

"If we return Telijencia to how it should

be, I'm sure we'll find him," replied Lucy, trying to be confident.

"Need to find that Juvitree first," said Awoo, perched on the front end of Lucy's slitherstick.

"Can hardly find you with that Cosmofobby thingy effect!" squawked Flewy, addressing Awoo to check that he was still flying alongside them.

"Is that better?" asked Lucy, as she and William reverted back from being chameleonised to normal and slowed down to a hover.

"Now what?" said Flewy, fully goggled, not wanting to linger. He was impatient to prove he was Supergull.

"We must organise our search, that's what!" replied William, crossly.

"Anyway, what does a stupid Juvitree look like?" asked Flewy.

Awoo put on his trying-to-be-wise look. "I should imagine it looks like some sort of tree."

"That's obvious!" squawked Flewy.

"Then you should be able to distinguish it from a toadstool," Awoo smirked.

"Quite," agreed Lucy, dismissively. "So if Awoo and Flewy fly clockwise around the perimeter of the lake and we go anti-clockwise, that way we'll..."

"Good idea except for the Awoo bit," interjected Flewy impudently. "He'll slow me down. Going in the backward direction with you is far more natural to him."

"...THAT way," Lucy continued firmly, "we'll automatically meet up and know who's found the Juvitree."

"I'm off then!" Flewy shot off like a rocket in the anti-clockwise direction and almost immediately flew back past them. "Oops, wrong way!" He screeched into the distance only to return again. "Which way is clockwise?" he asked, and looked at Awoo. "And I'm not asking you 'cos you'll get it wrong."

"That way," William pointed, "and be careful."

Awoo used his acute eyesight to help in

the search. Bravely, he would fly off Lucy's slitherstick from time to time and look closer at anything that had drawn their attention.

It was not long at all before Flewy unexpectedly returned, this time from the right direction. "Well go on, call me Mr Speedy!" he said hovering.

"Hello, Mr Weedy," hooted Awoo.

"Well I've been around the whole of the lake already," he boasted.

"Did you see anything?" asked Lucy.

"Forgot to look – I was going too fast," said Flewy.

"Then you'd better do it again but slower," said William firmly.

"Wait!" said Awoo, as something caught his eye. He flew off the slitherstick and swooped downwards to check it out. Flewy followed him closely, partly out of curiosity but mostly because he didn't want to go more slowly around the lake on his own.

"They must be Defenders," said Flewy, gliding alongside Awoo.

"Can't see any Juvitree," Awoo remarked.

Flewy purposely did what Awoo could not do and hovered above, but not too close, to the four uniformed, helmeted individuals. "Anybody seen a Juvitree?"

"I think it's Zag's screwy seagull wearing a funny hat," said Eraser, hiding his nose as he spoke to Shystar. "It might recognise me, so you speak to it!"

"Are you deaf down there?" squawked Flewy.

"Why?" asked Shystar.

"How should I know why you're deaf?" Flewy squawked, impatiently. "Must be your helmet!"

"Tell him where it is!" prompted Eraser, sharply.

Shystar pointed to the stump. "The only Juvitree is right here," he shouted, removing a chunk of fallen toadstool.

"I'll be back," squawked Flewy, as he and Awoo raced to tell the others.

"You get out there!" Eraser barked at Eilra. "Nala stays with me! So make sure you don't give the game away! And find out what's happening or else say good-bye to your dear little offspring!" he snarled, holding up the prismatran, showing two pathetic faces frozen in time, as an extra reminder before he hid out of sight.

Lucy and William flew cautiously towards the Juvitree as Flewy and Awoo directed them.

"Look, there's Eilra," said Awoo.

"We've done it, William!" Lucy gasped excitedly. "We've done it!"

"How's it you be flying 'bout on thum thar slithuursticks?" asked Eilra, greeting them, as Shystar helped them land. "An' where be Zag an' thum those eagles?"

"Thingummagadgeting," quipped Flewy, wanting to get on with it.

"This is my brother William, and we've come to return the Festalpod," smiled Lucy.

"Well I be thum dumbstruck, so I be overcome," gasped Eilra, fainting to the slimy ground.

Hidden from view, Eraser smirked with glee as Nala quivered next to him. "If that jerk was an actor, he'd win an Oscar for that performance!" he muttered, as the twins and the Eradicators tried to revive Eilra. "This brings matters to a head," he snarled. "As soon as Telijencia is restored, I'm in control of everything, including you! I want those Beautiflies caught and milked of all the ideas before they swarm. Do you understand?"

"An' you'll let us 'ave back our offspring?" Nala said trembling.

"All in good time," Eraser sneered. "Meanwhile get that overacting wally off the floor and remember, I'll be back!"

"They've got thum thar Festalpod, so I collapsed with surprise, I did furr sure," Eilra gasped, as Nala helped him to his feet and politely thanked everybody in the process.

"I thum noticed." She smiled at Lucy.

"Will I get an award from Astral for finding you first?" asked Flewy, buttering up to Shystar and impatient to get on with it.

"I saw them first!" Awoo hooted indignantly.

"You've got one already, twit-face!"

squawked Flewy, "AND anyway, I asked directions because you can't even hover... so that proves it!"

"Believe me, Astral will hear about it," replied Shystar. He hadn't seen the Festalpod and was dying to ask where it was, but was far too cunning to do so.

"Go on then, give it to them!" Flewy squawked at William.

"Actually, Lucy and I would like to put it in the Juvitree," said William.

"And so you should," smiled Shystar, "and I'm sure Eilra's recovered enough to show you how."

"It'll be me pleasure, so it will, 'tis furr sure," said Eilra, fully pleased with his performance.

"We'll take our leave and rejoin our craft," said Shystar. "But we will be back soon," he emphasised for the Rutilans' benefit.

"Pity you're not staying to see it all happen," said William.

"Duty calls, I'm afraid," replied Shystar.

"Remember my award," squawked Flewy. "I'll see you on the Island of Radiance in time for the party AND award ceremony."

"Of course," said Shystar, politely taking his leave with the other phoney Defenders to join Eraser in his hiding place behind the nearby spongy jagged rock and cluster of rotting giant fungi.

"That party sounds interesting," said Eraser.

"Must be the party Astral had us build that funfair for before we escaped and found you on the *Sea Err*," replied Shystar.

A sickly grin filled Eraser's helmet with evil. "Even more interesting," he muttered as Shystar waved at the periscope of the submerged but ever-watchful Camersible, signalling it to meet them further down the bank of the great lake.

Shystar looked back to see what was happening. "That stupid Seagull's even waving me goodbye," he mocked, returning a flippant salute and disappearing from view with Eraser.

"Right!" Flewy squawked, deciding he had shown enough courtesy to be recommended for an award, That's enough of the waving. Let's do it!" He suddenly realised the others were standing by the Juvitree. Awoo perched on William's shoulder as he was about to insert the Festalpod. "Hey! Hang on!" he screeched, zooming across to them, "I deserve to be in on this as well you know!"

"It don't look much now," said Nala, as they watched Eilra clear some fallen debris off the black, putrefied stump, "but when it awakens it's most beautiful."

"It's thur pointy end that goes in thum thar first, so 'tis," said Eilra, explaining to William and Lucy how to place the Festalpod in the core of the stump. "Before's yur do it, I tell yar all sorts of things'll 'appen, some scary like. But yar 'ave no need to worry 'cos ya'll come to no harm 'cos that's thur way it is furr certain."

Lucy and William proudly inserted the Festalpod, linking it into the taproot. They all stood back as it partially protruded from the core of the Juvitree-stump.

The crystal-blue planet of Cyan from the Constellation of Colour floated across the sky like a soap bubble as big as an ultra-gigantic moon. It sat in front of the bright golden sun, to tarry for a while and turn the sunrays green. For a moment all was serene and quiet like the calm before the storm, then the ground began to tremble as the Vernal Eclipse triggered the rejuvenation of the island.

Upon the lake, swirling fountains of rainbow-touched gushes pirouetted and twirled, dancing together like a company of ballet dancers performing a showcase of what was to be.

Wanting to share the wonders with Zag, William and Lucy picked up the slithersticks. But they had become brittle and fell apart in their hands.

Barefaced Cheek

Meanwhile, down in Lurkamungoo, a battle raged which prevented Zag from reaching the Globolloons.

He had managed to contain the advancing mass of Lurkwarriors by spraying them with Whodathawtit, an ecological de-icer invented to aid the Beamsurfer in cold climates. This Thingummagadgetal mixture had a base of red-hot chillies, salt and a dash of sherbet. It fizzled their sluglike skins making them itch like fury, and as they were unable to scratch themselves it was all the more irritating.

Arms firmly squelch-tied in knots, Gudorphal and Putridia had no option but to watch Gutrumble display a talent worthy of a Wimbledon tennis champion. As the Globlins splurted out of the oozing walls like squiggy missiles, he lobbed them with his great paws – but it was never-ending and he began to tire.

It was at this point of exhaustion, and when Zag was down to his last aerosol of Whodathawtit, that everything began to change. In mid-splurt, the Globlins innards burst out and their sac-skins fell to the ground, like popped balloons smeared with gunge. The mass of Lurkwarriors bubbled and squirmed as they dissolved to become a gurgling mess of horrid liquid. Ooze dripped off the pulsating walls like warm greasy fat, allowing steps of crystal-clear waterfalls to flow once more and wash away the slimy filth. Suckabogs evaporated leaving behind huge openings of freedom to the Telijencian sky.

An enormous burst of flatulence suddenly resounded throughout the cavern making Gutrumble all set to apologise. Realising it was the sound of the Putrisphere's vent flapping wildly he and Zag watched the whole monstrosity rapidly deflate to a quarter of its original size as it emitted an ear-piercing raspberry for its finalé. Bereft of their elasticity, the noise shattered the Globolloons like a soprano's pitch breaks wine glasses – and it rained Mogster-catpirates and two eagles.

"Hey Zag," grinned Gutrumble, "wuh makes a gweat team!" He put a grotty great paw on Zag's head. "Pity yuh body's missing though."

Catpone rushed over with Legs to look at the bodiless head. "Uh... is dat Zag or uh... elliptical confusion?"

"Optical illusion," Zag chuckled, unfastening his safety-pin, taking off his Invisibilising Sheet and putting his fez back on his head.

"It's Zag, yuh bwlock-head!" Legs mouthed.

Catpone looked puzzled. "Den he oughta be a uh... musician."

"Magician, Boss," corrected Gutrumble.

"Don't be stupid Guts, Zag's uh... Fingummamathematician," replied Catpone, proud he'd managed such a word.

"Thingummagadgetician, Boss," corrected Gutrumble, just as proudly.

A series of large crispy-brittle membrane curtains shattered one behind the other revealing a short, wide, sloping pathway up to the cavern's gaping entrance. Zag quickly made his way up the slope to see if there was any sign of William, Lucy, Flewy and Awoo.

He looked across the lake. The brilliant sun shone green on the swirling rainbow-tinted fountains of water which merged together as they built towards an awesome finale. It would not be long before a torrential idea storm rained vigorously upon the whole of Telijencia.

"I don't know what we'd do without you," smiled Eggna gratefully as she and Eggbert swooped down beside him.

"It's not me you should thank," said Zag worriedly, "it's the twins, Flewy and Awoo, who returned the Festalpod to the Juvitree."

Eggbert sensed Zag was troubled. "Where are they?"

"I'm hoping they'll return before the storm sets in," he sighed, "because without the Beamsurfer..."

"Come on Eggna," said Eggbert, "let's find them and bring them ba..."

"Aaaeeooooomm! ZZzzoooooom!" Flewy screeched overhead, with jet-fighter pilot delusions, doing a victory roll. "WHEY HEY! IT'S ME SUPERGULL AT YOUR SERVICE!" he said, landing and taking a bow.

Zag shook his head and grinned with relief. "And the others?"

"Their slithersticks fell apart," said Flewy, "they're waiting by the Juvitree. BUT it didn't take me long to find you lot," he boasted, puffing out his chest. "Oh by the way," he squawked, patting it, "NOTICE EVERYBODY PLEASE, there's plenty of room here for a big medal!"

"We're very grateful to ya, buddy," Eggbert smiled. "Maybe ya could take Eggna and I to fetch the twins and Awoo?" He winked at Zag. "And don't fly so fast we can't keep up with ya."

Pleased with the outcome, Zag watched out for their return as the gentle breeze fast gained pace and became a wind.

"Zag!" shouted Spooky. Without a trilby his ghostly white ears stood out prominently as he ran towards him. "Dere yuh are," he panted. "I've found yuh Beamsurfer an' duh crew's washing down it wiv dere shoiyts as a fank you."

Looking rather concerned about his craft's welfare, Zag quickly followed him. "That's very kind of them but..."

"Dat's okay, dere shoiyts badly needed a wash anyways," said Spooky kindly, "so dey're dipping dem in duh waterfall an' instead of wringing 'em out dey're using 'em tuh make it nice an' shiny again for yuh."

As they walked through Lurkamungoo, they watched its vileness disappearing fast. Already the cavern was being rejuvenated to a richness all of its own. Its rocky walls glistened with a spectacular range of coloured minerals and were patterned with veins of silver and gold. The boil-pumping rocks blossomed like sea anemones, purple, blue, crimson and white, yielding fragrances as fresh as mint, making the air clean like the dawning of a spring morning. The shrunken Putrisphere looked resplendent like a giant sea-urchin's shell made of pink granite and encrusted with vertical stripes of bobbled quartz. This once vile place had taken on a wondrous beauty even more colourful and spectacular than a coral reef teeming with life.

No longer blocked by a suckabog, the large opening above the Beamsurfer paid homage to the brilliant rays of vernal green sunshine. Zag's craft stood in a deep gully, gleaming like an emerald. His attention was drawn to something quite comical.

"I thought you said the crew were using their shirts, not their shorts," he gasped, staring at the sight of bare, furry bottoms of all shapes and sizes mooning at him as their upper halves polished away.

"Dat's wot I told yuh," said Spooky.

"Shoiyts."

"DON'T YUH DARE!" yelled Legs, arriving in time to stop Catpone from joining in. "DAT'S DISGUSTING! I just caught ya in duh nick'a time."

"Uh... don't be silly Legs... I don't wear knickers," replied Catpone, dodging a clout across the ear.

"WHO YUH CALLING SILLY?" Not one to give up easily, Legs caught him with a swift follow up. "I can't leave yuh side wivout yuh acting der TWERP!" She grabbed hold of him and led him away like a naughty little boy. "Guts wants a word wiv yuh, and den SO DO I!"

"Uh, Boss," said Gutrumble, standing over Gudorphal and Putridia, as Legs placed a meek-looking Catpone beside him.

"I'll be back!" Legs clipped him one for luck. "So behave while I go tuh wait for my kitties!"

"She's so uh... attwactive whun she gets angwy," sighed Catpone, watching her dreamily a she walked away.

"Uh, BOSS!" said Gutrumble, making him jump. "Wot shall I do wiv dis pair of blubber-bags?"

"Put 'em on duh uh... me-an-you for duh award party."

"Menu, Boss," corrected Gutrumble.

"Dat's wot I said!" replied Catpone.

Metamorphosis!

Zag was trying to repair the broken-down Beamsurfer. It was gleaming but, until Zag could fix it, it was stranded under the same large opening where the Mogsters had polished it. He had just replaced the reverse-thrust processor and a few fuses, when there was a knock on the cockpit door. His bearded face beamed a million smiles as he saw the twins and Awoo.

"All present and correct," grinned Eggbert, as Zag jumped down to give Lucy and William a big cuddle, "so I'll leave ya to it." Acknowledging Zag's wink of thanks, he added, "The storm's brewing up nicely, so if ya want to see it, don't be long."

"Am I proud of you all or am I proud of you all?" chuckled Zag. "You deserve to be very proud of yourselves."

Lucy gave Zag a squeeze. "Have you got

the Beamsurfer working?"

"I was just about to find out," Zag smiled, "so hop in and let's see." It was then he realised someone was missing. "Where's Flewy?"

"Need you ask," Awoo hooted sardonically. "Supermouth's perched on a rock surrounded by Mogsters, beaking about how he single-handedly saved them all from Globscurity!"

"And we'll be lucky if that's the last we hear of it," laughed William.

"Oh, and you'd better have this back," said Lucy, sitting next to Zag and handing him back his Cosmo-fob.

"You keep it," he smiled, fiddling with the controls. "I'll make myself another when I get back to my barn." Zag pressed a button and flicked some switches. The Beamsurfer coughed and spluttered then whirred softly like a muffled hairdryer. "It works!" He grinned at the sound of applause then shut down the power unit.

"Maybe the Cosmoputa will work, now there's no suckabog to block the signal," suggested William.

"Good thought," said Zag. "That's my next task. I ought to contact Astral." He gave it a try but nothing happened. Adjusting his half-rimmed glasses he identified what was wrong. "The Fibrostatic Sensor Root is loose. Ah well, if he's on Telijencia, he'll probably meet up with us after the storm."

"If he is on the island, he'll be on his own," said Lucy. "His Defenders waved good-bye to us."

"That's right," added William, "they said that duty called."

"Not before Flewy made sure they'd get Astral to give him an award at the party," Awoo chipped in disparagingly.

"He'll never change," Zag chuckled.

"I wondered where muh kitties had got tuh!" Legs' face beamed through the cockpit door. "Eggbert says yuh oughta come and see duh rejuvithingy storm."

"Coming," smiled Lucy.

"I'll fix the Cosmoputa later," said Zag, suddenly finding that he was the last to leave the Beamsurfer. He had to catch up the others as they followed Legs to the mouth of the cavern. "What happened to Eilra and Nala?" he puffed as he caught up with them.

"They said they had to prepare for the Beautiflies and would join us as soon as they could," replied William.

"How do they know where we are?" Zag asked as they reached the front of the huge entrance.

"Flewy or Eggbert must have told them, I suppose," replied William, distracted by the final build-up of the tornado.

It was a truly magnificent sight. The centre of the great lake erupted into a spiralling tower of water and the brilliant green sun shone directly above it, sending an emerald shaft down into its core. At the same time the sky changed to yellow, then red, then blue, turning the silvery twisting tower into a vast rippling pillar of resplendent light. It kept growing in height until it touched the sky, then with a whoosh formed a black mushroom cloud that surged and spread to darken the whole island.

The storm was set to hit Telijencia. A tremendous electric charge THUNDER-BOOMED through the air causing Flewy to scuttle for cover under Zag's coat-tails. The cloud burst, pouring torrents of sparkling rain upon the land.

Flewy cautiously beaked his way out. "Ju.. just thought I'd lost something," he squeaked in embarrassment, knowing superheroes didn't do that sort of thing.

Nobody had noticed, all eyes were fixed in amazement at the sight on the tranquil shimmering lake – the *Mobsea Dick* had risen to the surface. More pristine than ever before, its masts stood proud on the galleon as it glinted in the bright sunshine, winking a deluge of welcomes to the gob-smacked Mogster crew.

"YAR MUST HURRY, so yar should!" shouted Eilra, as he and Nala suddenly came running towards the entrance.

"What's the problem?" asked Zag.

"Thar strong flush-current will take yur

ship into thum thar sea," Nala puffed.

Panting, Eilra put his hands on his knees. "Yar need t'git on board before thum thar mountain opens up, so be it very soon."

The Mogsters rushed down to the side of the lake before Eilra could fully catch his breath.

"Wait a minute, you lot!" Zag called out. "Somebody stop them! They could be drowned by the flush-current!"

Flewy took off after them like a rocket. "STOP! STOP!" he shrieked, hovering above the Mogsters and grabbing their attention so that Zag and the twins could catch up.

"Gather around quickly," said Zag, rummaging in his Thingummajacket. In keen anticipation, Catpone and his crew encircled Zag as he took out a bag filled with small brownish cubes and offered them around.

Catpone took a pawful greedily to fill his mouth. "Hey uh fanks, Zag."

"DON'T EAT THEM!" Zag yelled, stopping him just in time. "It's not fudge! They're my Flingummadinghies."

The Mogsters looked at him as if he were potty. Zag looked back as if he wasn't and demonstrated by carefully putting a cube in the water. It immediately expanded into a dinghy with room enough for two – except for Gutrumble who would almost fill one up all on his own.

Zag stepped into the water and showed them a tag dangling at the 'blunt end'. "Pull this and there will be enough Jetti-thrust to reach your ship. You steer it by leaning to the left or right." He'd hardly finished his instructions when the Mogsters chucked their cubes in the lake. The Flingummadinghies inflated, shot back up through the surface of the water and high into the air, then landed on the Mogsters like a downpour of large tractor-tyre inner-tubes. Bashed but unperturbed, Catpone and his crew grabbed the dinghies and jumped into them like demented Formula-1 drivers late for the start of the Grand Prix.

"IGNORWANT GIT, CATPONE!" bawled an angry, forgotten Legs.

"Here, get in mine, Legs," Spooky offered, bowing like a gentleman, accepting her smile and smartly assisting her aboard.

In rapid succession Jetti-thrust tags were located, then pulled, and the lake threw surging waves in the wake of each and every Mogster's enthusiasm to reach the galleon first.

"My bet's on Spooky and Legs," grinned Eggbert, putting a wing around Eggna as they joined Zag and the twins on the bank of the lake, watching the Mogsters race towards the *Mobsea Dick*.

"I taught Spooky to steer straight," said Awoo, proudly, perching on Zag's shoulder and puffing out his chest.

"So you did." Zag smiled, but only for a moment. A sudden series of rumblings warned them that the mountain gorge was beginning to part. Zag turned around to ask Eilra and Nala how much rock disturbance it would cause, but they had gone. Concerned that the quaking activity might harm the Beamsurfer sitting in the gully, he decided to return to his craft immediately. He swiftly reached inside his Thingummajacket, then gave two Jetticans to Eggbert.

"Take these with Eggna and replace the old ones on the *Mobsea Dick*," Zag suggested. "They will help make sure the Mogsters get back to the Island of Radiance at speed and in one piece."

"You sure you will be okay?" Eggna asked.

"We'll be fine," Zag nodded. "The twins, Flewy, Awoo and I will follow in the Beamsurfer."

"But ya Beamsurfer doesn't work," said Eggbert.

"Zag's fixed it," said William, proudly.

"Okay, then I guess that's it," smiled Eggbert.

"Take care, and see ya later!" Eggna called back as they flew off towards the galleon.

Zag, the twins, Flewy and Awoo swiftly made their way through the cavern to the Beamsurfer.

"Look at that!" exclaimed Lucy.

They paused briefly to look at the buckled skeleton of the Cameracraft, set in the rock and laid bare by the disappearance of the slime.

"The Lurks must have had Eraser!" gasped William.

"Let's hope so," said Zag thoughtfully, recalling his previous adventure, when he had stood on the deck of the *Sea Err* with Astral, watching Eraser trying to escape in the Cameracraft and crashing into the sea.

Another rumble resounded throughout the cavern. "Don't hang about!" squawked

Flewy, as he and Awoo flew across to the Beamsurfer.

They followed immediately and climbed aboard. Small stones trickled onto the craft from the top of the rocky gully that had once been filled by the suckabog. Zag shut the cockpit door. "Let's go to the Juvitree, we will be safe from falling rocks," he said, starting the power source and checking all the seat-belts were fastened. "I'll fix the Cosmoputa there."

The Beamsurfer whirred into life and Zag carefully manoeuvred it out of the jagged gap and up into the clear blue sky.

Hovering high above the island, they saw the *Mobsea Dick* billowing in full sail. Assisted by the strong current it was making swift headway through the gap and into the sparkling blue Ocean of Creativity. At the port and starboard of the *Mobsea Dick* shimmering waterfalls dropped like feathered curtains of wind-ruffled, silver-green satin, a spectacle fit for a royal coronation.

From their bird's-eye view the splendour

of the island was clear, and it showed how the great lake filled the deep valley in the mountains. The fungi jungle had been replaced by a lush forest which swept around the slopes of the lake, over the hills and down to golden sandy beeches, scattered with palm trees.

"It's down there!" said Flewy impatiently, pointing in the direction of the Juvitree, wanting to get this over with and collect his award.

Zag landed the Beamsurfer on the banks by the Juvitree. Even Flewy gasped at its beauty.

The black putrefied stump had become a rich golden colour, rippled with streaks of silver and pearly quartz. A profusion of thick- stemmed tropical leaves, intermingled with sparkling blue and white blossom, splayed a lush petal-like coronet around the rim. No longer dormant, the Juvitree looked like a magnificent green and golden crown encased with jewels. The last of the bright-blue and white-striped Beetapillars were wriggling away to lap up the idea-globules, glistening succulent droplets left by the rainstorm on the luxuriant vegetation – it was even more wonderful than Astral had described to Zag.

"I'd better fix this Cosmoputa," said Zag. "Its Fibrostatic Sensor Root has come loose."

He pointed to a compartment in front of Lucy's seat. "If you open that you'll see two sachets of Nebulostic Suspension Gel with NSG Fixing Solution, could you pass them to me please?"

Thanking Lucy, he reinserted the Fibrostatic Sensor Root into the Purple Centrifugal Novacrystal, the Cosmoputa's purple saucer-sized disc with a hole in the middle, then carefully added the fixing solution. "Let's hope that doesn't come loose again."

Like a genie gushing out of a bottle, a spherical holographic, silvery mist appeared, soft-lit, and encapsulated in a laser-like network of tinted purple light. "I've fixed it," Zag grinned happily like the cheekiest of bears with a bucket of honey, while the twins and Awoo marvelled at the vista-globe.

Annoyingly, Flewy tapped a bored wing on the back of Zag's seat. "Come on, let's go!" he squawked, impatiently.

Suddenly Eilra and Nala appeared from behind the lush Juvitree and Zag jumped out of the Beamsurfer to meet them.

"Yar must leave before thum thar Beautiflies swarm, lest yur craft damages thum an' thar be no good at all, so it won't," said Eilra. "It be our busy time, so 'tis."

"Yar can watch it from thar sky but not furr too long," added Nala, kindly.

"Of course," said Zag, feeling a little hurried. "Have you seen Astral?"

"We bumped into the Defenders further down the shore and they told us to tell yar that they'd see yar soon," replied Eilra.

"At the party!" Flewy's beak poked out of the Beamsurfer's cockpit door.

"How long ago did you see them?" asked Zag.

"Never mind about that, Zag!" squawked Flewy, "We'll miss the PARTY! Now let's go, PLEASE!"

Eilra looked impatient. "Thar's right, you don't wanna do that so thanks furr everything, an' 'ave a good journey, good-bye we says."

"They're rather cool towards us now everything's all right," Lucy commented as Zag jumped aboard and closed the door.

"Look, they've gone already," said William, in an irritated voice, "and haven't even waved us good-bye."

"Must have spent too much time with Flewy," Awoo quipped.

"Fasten your seat belts," Zag intervened. "Well, I suppose it is their busy time," he added as they took off.

"Now what?" asked Flewy irately, as yet again they hovered over the middle of the lake.

"That's what!" said Awoo, as the mountain closed to seal the lake.

"And that's so beautiful!" gasped Lucy,

pointing at the bedazzling cloudlike mass of colour, fluttering and swirling back to the Juvitree.

"Beautiflies with silken wings," said Zag, in sheer wonderment. "Their metamorphosis is complete and this must be their final display of brilliance." Zag opened the observation window to listen to them buzzing with rejuvenated ideas. For a few short moments they shared the telescope to watch them.

"L...LOOK AT THAT!" exclaimed William, in utter amazement.

Out of the sunny green sky a rainbow touched the Juvitree, signifying all was at peace, and the season of rejuvenation nearly over.

"Now that is the ethereal pathway to the Constellation of Colour, the place from where every rainbow is sent," Zag explained. "Astral told me that from all across the island the Beautiflies return to the Juvitree, swarm into the rainbow and migrate to the Constellation of Colour. It's by this means that the ideas are redistributed into the Galaxy of Ideas for the benefit of all creativity."

"Can we cut the second-hand science lesson?" Flewy squawked, impudently. "I know all I need to... the twins get it in school... and Awoo's to dumb to understand anyway!"

"All you know is how to be extremely rude!" Awoo hooted. "After all you are SUPERPLONKER!"

"I'm not even sure whether we should allow him to go to the party," said Lucy.

"Let's ask Eggbert to deal with him," suggested William.

"I'll be good... honest!" squeaked Flewy.

Zag was mindful of what Eilra had warned. "It's time to go back to the Island of Radiance, folks."

"AND ABOUT TIME TOO!" squawked Flewy, totally unable to keep his beak shut. "OOPS!" he added, quickly. "S...sorry it's my bad habit... don't worry, I'll tell myself off."

A Nice Surprise?

It took no time at all for the Beamsurfer to reach the Island of Radiance. Zag slowed down as they flew over the lagoon. The *Sea Err* was anchored in the same position as when he'd left, still canopied in submarine mode and separate from its carrier-deck.

What did surprise them all was seeing the *Mobsea Dick* already at its harbour moorings. The Rutilans had been very busy while the Mogsters had been away. The wooden quay had been repaired and was festooned with balloons. "That's the last thing I wanted to see," joked William, as Zag prepared to land.

"We'd better sort out some clean clothes," Zag said to the twins.

"You all look clean enough to me," remarked Awoo. It was true, and only then did any of them have the time to notice.

"WICKED! Must have been the rejuve-nation effects of Telijencia," said William, cheerfully.

"Hope it's done the same for Gutrumble," laughed Lucy, glad her favourite jeans hadn't been ruined.

The cockpit door had hardly opened when Flewy shot out, nearly crashing into Eggbert, and squawked, "I'm off to find Astral!"

"You were quick!" Zag chuckled, as he and the others got out of the Beamsurfer.

"Ya Jetticans worked really well, like rockets," Eggbert smiled, glad to see them safe, "and I mean REALLY well... that's why!" He smoothed his brow with a wing. "Boy oh boy... tha' was some trip!"

Awoo recalled how peaceful the *Mobsea Dick's* crow's-nest had been. "If you'll excuse me folks, I'm going to get some shut-eye," he said, flying off. "See you later."

"See ya pal," said Eggbert, as Zag and the twins jumped down out of the Beamsurfer to join the eagle.

Zag shut the cockpit door, and smiled at Lucy and William. "You two go on ahead, I'll catch up with you shortly."

Zag and Eggbert stood a little way from the quayside and quietly watched the hive of activity. Legs was yelling, organising the Mogsters, the scores of Rutilans and anybody else she could muster to help with the preparations for the award ceremony.

"Best place to be, I reckon," said a familiar voice, coming from behind them. "And you've done brilliantly!"

Zag turned and smiled. "Astral! At last we meet!" he said, as they all greeted each other warmly.

"Well, I saw Telijencia had been restored, spoke to Eilra and Nala, then I came straight here."

"We're ready! We're ready!" squawked Flewy. "We're waiting for Astral to arri... Nice to see you, Sir! S...see you on board." He saluted then zoomed back to the *Mobsea Dick*.

"He's being very polite today," laughed

Astral.

"He wants an award," smiled Zag.

"He has been very brave in helping us," added Eggbert, putting in a quick 'word' on his behalf.

"I know," Astral sighed, "I left his name off the communication I sent to Zag. I meant to mention him along with the twins and Awoo."

"Looks like they're waving at us to go aboard," laughed Eggbert.

The tropical evening was setting in as they approached the *Mobsea Dick*. Zag noticed the new sign by the gangway and gave a sigh of relief.

LURPS OFF DA MEAN YOU PRIVET FANKSHUN SO GIT LOST!!

The streamers decorating the main deck fluttered in the breeze in unison with the parasols on each table. Gutrumble looked repulsively splendid with his fat fur-matted gut bursting out of his chef's outfit. He busied himself at the top table, fussing around the twins, Flewy and Awoo as they sat waiting for Zag and Astral to join them.

"He's not the chef is he?" gulped Lucy, as Gutrumble walked out of earshot.

"See!" squawked Flewy. "Just like I said before we came here!"

"What's on the menu?" asked William.

"That's the problem," Lucy grimaced. "There is no menu."

"Salmonella pie, probably!" quipped Flewy.

"Not a problem for you then," said Awoo. "I thought you liked fish?"

"Thinking is definitely not your strong point," replied Flewy, beak-smiling at Astral and Zag as at last they joined him and the others at the top table.

"Hope you're behaving yourself, Flewy," grinned Astral. "By the way, I do like your fancy-dress outfit."

The whole top table vibrated with giggles as Flewy flipped up his goggles. For once he thought better of saying anything rude, so as not to jeopardise his award. "Thank you," he replied most graciously.

"Creep," Awoo whispered to Flewy. Just then, Legs Diamonté appeared as if from nowhere and grabbed the attention of the guests at every table on the main deck.

A few of the Mogster crew climbed the rigging for a better view, their full vision having been somewhat blocked by the main mast. The Rutilan guest fraternity 'tut-tutted' at such unruly behaviour – bad manners and all that. Even so, more of the Mogsters climbed the rigging and Spooky let out a wolf-whistle which, upon reflection, seemed rather odd for a panther-like cat.

Legs looked ever so beautiful in a glittering blue evening-gown set off by her sleek white fur. Her manicured claws matched the colour of her dress and daintily pointed Zag and Astral to sit at the centre of the top table.

"You do look gorgeous," Lucy complimented her.

"Thanks kitty," she smiled, making way for Catpone's announcement.

Catpone fiddled with his eye-patch, adjusted his new trilby, then walked from the main mast to the top table. Without further ado, he thumped the table hard with his big, grotty paw. Flewy jumped, knocked over a jug of water, and Awoo got very wet. Regardless, Catpone banged the table again just to make certain every guest was brought to order and was listening. "UH... BE UH... DOWNSITTING!"

"Upstanding, Boss," corrected Gutrumble, who was now standing beside him.

"Uh whatever... Guts," Catpone cleared his throat. "I pwesent Astwal who'll dish out duh uh...warts."

"Awards, Boss," corrected Gutrumble.

Astral stood up to a warm reception, raised his hand and waited for the applause to die down. "Please save it for my brave and kind friends, for it is they who deserve it." He smiled at Zag to stand up. "I have great pleasure, on behalf of my master, His Eminence The   Master of Creativity, Ruler of the Galaxy of Ideas, to bestow upon Zagwitz the Thingummagadgetician the Order of Ingenuity, and thereby appoint him Fellow of the Galactic Circle. And to give him the Freedom of the World of Creativity and the Galaxy of Ideas."

"I'd like to meet the Master," Lucy whispered to William. "I wonder where he lives and what he looks like?"

The clapping and banging on tables continued as Astral placed a golden sign of infinity around Zag's neck. Shaped like a flat, stretched figure eight and about ten centimetres in length, the pendant had a glowing red crystal at the cross-over point of the figure. Zag wore it with great pride.

"Welcome to our Galaxy," smiled Astral. "You have the right to enter our Inner Sanctum and sit around the Galactic Circle alongside other esteemed members who are dedicated to protecting and developing the wonders of creativity. You are truly our supreme friend; the Master will welcome you always."

Zag bowed, knowing this honour to be of great importance. It was the key to the Galaxy of Ideas which would allow him to enter a world which was beyond normal imagination.

William clasped Lucy's hand. "Maybe we will meet the Master one day, now Zag has this award," he replied, intuitively.

"SPEECH! SPEECH!" someone shouted and Flewy gave them a stern look.

"A big thank you to all," said Zag. "We have become great friends, all of us, united by adversity. When I first came here, the Island was called Blot, but now it flourishes as the Island of Radiance. During those terrible times we all played our part in vanquishing Eraser The Terrible..."

Zag paused to let the applause die down.

"...Little did I or Lucy, William, Awoo or Flewy, realise that coming here to receive our awards would land us in yet another adventure. Maybe it will be a holiday next time we visit..."

This time the applause was mixed with laughter and Zag paused once more to let it die down.

"Now Telijencia is also restored..."

Even more applause and banging of tables interrupted his flow, but he smiled and waited patiently.

"...Forgotten ideas will be rejuvenated once more, but let us make sure those ideas are used as gifts to be nurtured for the good of all and not for greed and evil." Zag held up his pendant. "Thank you, Astral, for bestowing such an honour upon me and thank you all for being my friends."

Zag sat down, much to Flewy's relief, and to huge applause and banging of tables.

"Thank you Zagwitz." Astral smiled and continued, "For their bravery and courage, and their example of friendship and support, I also have great pleasure, on behalf of his Eminence The Master of Creativity, Ruler of the Galaxy of Ideas, in awarding Lucy, William, Awoo and Flewy the Freedom of the Island of Radiance for all they did to help us fight Eraser in those dark times. And, for all they have done on this visit in helping find Telijencia, they are formally recognised by these pendants as Honoured Members of the World of Creativity and the Galaxy of Ideas."

As the applause began again, Astral gave each of them a certificate and carefully placed a silver sign of infinity around each of their necks. The pendants were approximately half the size of Zag's and each had a white crystal set into the cross-over point of the figure.

Lucy and William faced the audience and the applause died down as everybody waited for them to say something. It was at that point the twins found the whole experience nerve-wracking and they stared in silence, feeling very conspicuous indeed.

"G...go on s...say something..." whispered William nervously. "Y...you're the e...eldest."

"Only by a few minutes," Lucy muttered to him, realising that William had momentarily dried up. "W...we are very privileged and... would like to thank you for being our friends... for this lovely party..." Lucy blushed like mad, froze, and couldn't think what to say next, "and ... and..."

"And we'd like to thank the Mogsters for not eating Flewy and Awoo when we first came here at the time of Blot," added William, totally surprised at the way his mouth had suddenly taken the initiative.

"Thank you Astral and everybody," smiled Lucy as she and William sat down at their table to the sound of clapping and laughter. "And thank you LITTLE brother for putting me on the spot," she scolded.

"Got you out of it though, sis," retorted William, as Awoo, being much too private to do anything but wave a grateful wing, gave Flewy his opportunity to become the centre of attention.

"At least this fits," squawked Flewy, undiplomatically, with his pendant around his neck and still fully goggled in his red helmet. "Now I remember, that is before I became Supergull…"

"DUH MEAL'S SERVED!" shouted Gutrumble, as some of the Mogster crew rushed out carrying platters full of baked salmon and cream buns, and buckets of baked beans.

"…thanks anyway," squeaked Flewy, seeing everybody was far more interested in tucking into the meal.

"It's good food," whispered Astral to the twins as he sat next to them. "I made sure my Defenders brought it here… but I had to promise Gutrumble we'd include baked beans."

Lucy and William giggled at the thought.

"Spooky will love you!" Zag chuckled at Astral.

At the close of the meal the sky suddenly lit up with fireworks. Lucy and William rushed to the side of the galleon to see what was happening. A big ferris-wheel was lit up behind the palms and turned slowly against the darkening sky. Crowds of Rutilans were streaming towards it.

"We arranged a funfair especially for this occasion," said a Defender, standing beside them. "Come on, I'll show you."

The twins looked across at Zag and Astral who were deeply engrossed in conversation.

"Okay, but not for long," said Lucy. Awoo flew down beside them. "Do you want to come to the funfair?" she asked.

"Not my scene thanks," replied Awoo, yearning for some peace and quiet after all their adventures.

"Tell Zag where we are," said William as they dashed off.

Zag was still busy chatting and Flewy continued to show off his award and entertain some Mogsters with fables of his heroism. Awoo flew back to the crow's-nest for another rest.

Zag and Astral were far too engrossed with their discussion to notice anything around them.

"...but there can't have been Defenders on

Telijencia," Astral insisted. "We searched and searched everywhere but we couldn't find or contact you."

As Lucy and William arrived at the glittering funfair a huge steam-driven organ belched out a hazy colourful mist, hissing a tune which heralded the entrance to fun.

"Look Lucy, a Ghost Train!" shouted William in excitement.

"ROLL UP! ROLL UP! All aboard the Ghost Train!" shouted a tall spindly clown with a sickly grin and funny long, red-painted nose.

"Come on, let's try it," said William, tugging Lucy towards the clown.

"First two get a special ride!" the clown called out. "You can ride on the footplate with me and I'll show you how an old steam engine works."

"Cor that'll be cool, won't it, Lucy?" said William.

"No!" replied Lucy sharply, with no enthusiasm whatsoever.

"Why not?" asked William in an irritated

voice as she pulled him away.

"He seems weird, and sort of reminds me of someone tall and nasty," she said, beginning to run away.

"Of course he's weird, he's a clown!" called out William, angrily running after her and catching her up.

There were too many Defenders in the way for the clown to chase them. He watched them run away, leant against a lever and the engine let off a dirty black cloud of steam.

"I said that man reminded me, that's all!" Lucy panted, as they quickly reached the quay.

The *Mobsea Dick*'s pontoon was crowded with well-wishers; Zag and Astral were bustling their way down the gangway with Flewy in his element hovering and squawking above them.

"There's no way we'll get through that lot," said Lucy, waving frantically to catch Astral and Zag's attention. "Best we wait for them here on the quayside," she said, tugging

William's arm to make him stop.

"We were coming to look for you!" Astral called out, as he and Zag continued to shake hands with all and sundry.

Still livid at missing his ride on the Ghost Train, William took no notice of the well-meant commotion. "Hang on, Lucy! You thought that clown was Eraser, didn't you? Well that's really stupid! Eraser doesn't exist any more, you know that! You saw his wrecked Cameracraft on Telijencia."

"And I'm not stupid!" Lucy fumed.

"Okay! Sorry!" puffed William. "But he's probably one of Astral's Defenders."

"I don't care," said Lucy, "I didn't like him, SO stop keeping on about it!"

"Noisy lot!" hooted Awoo, swooping over the twins' heads and making his way to the Beamsurfer.

Lucy and William were immediately enveloped by a mass of guests all trying to say good-bye.

"Hope tuh seeya soon muh kitties," shouted Legs, blowing a big kiss at the twins.

Astral bent down and whispered in Zag's ear, "We must talk very soon, then meet at the Galactic Circle."

"I'll contact you as soon as Lucy and William's parents have picked them up," Zag nodded.

By the time Zag, the twins and Flewy had said yet another round of handshaking goodbyes to the Mogsters and the many Rutilan guests who wanted to congratulate them, they were covered in streamers, and exhausted.

"And not before time too," hooted Awoo, as Zag opened the door of the Beamsurfer and they all climbed aboard to surf the beam back to Zag's barn.

Who Set the Alarm?

It was just as well Zag hadn't dozed off like the others, as the Beamsurfer sped through the galaxies to arrive back at his barn at the exact time in the evening as they had left.

But now it was morning and the twins were still fast asleep in Zag's bedsit loft, as was Awoo high up in the barn. Zag was snoring, his head resting on his Thinking-Pad desk where, in the early hours, he'd sat quietly with much to consider and had inadvertently fallen fast asleep.

Even the bright sunshine hadn't roused any of them – that is except for Flewy. "Waaark! Waaark!" he squawked, "TIME TO WAKE UP! TIME TO WAKE UP! The twins' parents are here!"

Zag woke up with a jolt and straightened his Thingummajacket's lapels. "Heavens, it's nine o'clock already," he gasped, blearily checking his watch then rushing into the barn.

In no time at all the barn was a hive of activity. Lucy clattered down the ladder from the bed-sit loft, swiftly followed by William.

"MORNING ALL," Zag shouted, as he searched around the barn. "Anybody seen my fez?"

"STOP MAKING SO MUCH NOISE ALL OF YOU!" hooted Awoo, swooping down from his quarters, commendably sacrificing his owl-sleep routine to say a polite 'hello'. "Where are they, Flewy?" he asked, not seeing a parent in sight and perching on a beam to avoid the frantic goings-on.

"JUST JOKING!" squawked Flewy, between practising somersaults as he hovered close by in the air.

"No matter, they'll be here in an hour or two," Zag said, quickly averting a bird quarrel and ruffling his white hair with his fingers. "At least we now have time for breakfast."

"BREAKFAST!" Awoo hooted angrily. "It's SLEEP I need!"

"We've found it!" William called out.

Lucy handed the fez to Zag. "It was in the Beamsurfer."

"Glad to see you're both dressed," said Zag, thanking Lucy and adjusting the fez on his head. "Although it looks as if neither of you got undressed," he added with a grin. It was true that the twins hadn't, having dozed off during the return journey, then spent much of the night lying on their bunk bed chatting to each other about their adventure, before finally dropping off to sleep.

Zag set the rickety table in the centre of the barn, William drew up some boxes to sit on and Lucy made toast. They were soon eating breakfast and washing it down with orange juice and coffee.

Zag had firmly given Flewy the choice between sitting at the table or losing his Antiwobble-finthruster. Flewy had taken the first option. Awoo joined them, deciding there was no point in him going back to sleep to have to get up again soon, so he made his presence felt by yawning frequently.

"So tell me," Zag asked the twins as he munched a piece of toast, "did you both enjoy the funfair?"

"Lucy was scared of a clown," William sniggered.

"So!" said Lucy, embarrassed and angry that the fact had been mentioned.

"May I ask why?" said Zag.

"She thought he was Eraser," William spluttered with laughter, nearly choking on his cereal.

"I never said that!" Lucy fumed at William, feeling stupid. She refilled her glass with orange juice.

"Did he have a long nose?" yawned Awoo.

"He did actually," Lucy replied confidently, the question having made her feel not quite so ridiculous.

"Doesn't mean a thing, twit-head," chipped in Flewy. "Clowns wear false noses."

"You should know!" Awoo quipped

with a yawn.

Zag was intrigued. A number of things hadn't added up and such matters had been on his mind when he'd fallen asleep at his desk. Between sips of coffee he related to them the conversation he had with Astral towards the end of the party...

"...but we did see Defenders on Telijencia," said William.

"I spoke to them," said Flewy. "One even mentioned the party."

"Then why did Astral insist his men hadn't been there?" Lucy queried. "Because they weren't there, they couldn't locate Telijencia until after its rejuvenation," Zag replied.

"You might not have seen them, but us four did," said Awoo, supported by the rare and fervent nods of agreement from Flewy.

"I'm not doubting you in the slightest," said Zag. "But neither do I doubt Astral."

"I'm far too sleepy for riddles," yawned Awoo.

"Eilra and Nala saw them too," said

William, wiping his mouth with his hand.

"Come to think of it, they were rather cool towards us after the island was rejuvenated," Lucy commented.

"Yeah," said William. "They were in such a hurry to leave they didn't even wave us good-bye."

"I suppose that could be viewed as a bit odd after all the help they gave us," said Zag, finishing his coffee and placing his mug on the table.

"After all the help we gave them," squawked Flewy, "it's VERY RUDE more like."

"And there speaks the expert!" yawned Awoo.

"Well, we'd better clear away this lot before your parents arrive," said Zag getting up from the table. "I'll be seeing Astral soon, there must be a simple explanation," he added, making light of it all and disguising his true feelings.

"Can we come with you when you do?" asked William.

"First, you need to go home. Second, I need to visit the Inner Sanctum and sit with Astral at the Galactic Circle. And thirdly..." Zag smiled. "I am sure after that I can arrange something."

"If at all possible," said Lucy, excitedly, starting to clear away the breakfast debris, "we'd love to meet the Master."

"I'd love your parents to hurry up so I can get some sleep," Awoo yawned.

"And we'd love to visit the Constellation of Colours," added William, about to pick up the box he'd been sitting on.

"From now on, I wouldn't be surprised if every rainbow was filling our world with ideas," said Lucy, picking up some dishes.

"You'd be surprised if Eraser was on the other end of it," squawked Flewy.

Four pairs of eyes stared daggers at him.

"I was joking," Flewy squeaked.

"You are a pathetic joke!" hooted Awoo.

For a brief moment Zag went deep into thought, then quickly became aware of the stony silence. "Come on you lot," he smiled,

"I need to tidy this place up before your parents arrive."

"Fat chance!" hooted Awoo, "That's the one thing you're incapable of doing."

"Just you watch me!" chuckled Zag, reaching inside his Thingummajacket.

Poppy

BY AVI

It's not always easy being brave - especially if you are a deer mouse and only six inches long (and three inches of that is your tail). Nevertheless, Poppy, with her beautiful orange-brown fur and dark round eyes is forced through necessity to become braver than any other mouse. She and her family live on the edge of the sprawling, sinister Dimwood Forest. They are ruled over by Mr Ocax, a great horned owl who dwells in Dimwood. But the mice are not just his subjects. They are also his dinners …

Deftly mixing humour, horror and pathos, Poppy is a colourful, memorable journey of courage and self-discovery. It is the first of four gripping books that make up the *Dimwood Forest Chronicles*.

ISBN 0 689 83651 1

Poppy and Rye

BY AVI

Saddened by the death of her friend Ragweed, Poppy once again journeys through the vast, dark Dimwood Forest to bring the tragic news to Ragweed's family.

But when Poppy and her prickly pal, Ereth the porcupine, arrive they find Ragweed's family already in turmoil. The quiet serene valley where Ragweed lived has been flooded by beavers, and the mice must move for fear of drowning.

Together Poppy and Rye – Ragweed's brother – face kidnapping, imprisonment, and even death in their struggle to save the mice. Will they succeed and defeat the beavers? And will Rye manage to step out of Ragweed's shadow and prove himself worthy of Poppy's love?

This is the second book of the *Dimwood Forest Chronicles*

ISBN 0 689 83667 8

MOONSILVER

KATHLEEN DUEY

Heart has no family. Found abandoned as a baby, she now lives a hard and lonely life in the dusty village of Ash Grove. Then one day she finds a scarred, skinny horse in the forest. Against the wishes of her mean-spirited guardian, Simon, Heart adopts the mare and names her Avamir.

When she realises Avamir is in foal, Heart is thrilled. And so too is Simon – now he has two horses he can sell to the slaughter-house instead of one. But when the colt is born, Heart finds him weak and with a strange bump on his forehead. A bump that begins to crack open, to reveal a silver point beneath ...

Heart realises that the horses are actually unicorns, magical creatures from ancient legend. But why are they here? If the unicorns aren't led away from Ash Grove they will surely be captured and killed by the superstitious villagers. Can Heart find a way to protect them, and the only love she has ever known?

Moonsilver is the first book in this
exciting new series *– The Unicorn's Secret*

ISBN 0 689 83675 9

Frindle

by Andrew Clements

Nick Allen – Troublemaker?

Nick says no. He just likes to liven things up at school, that's all – and he's always full of great ideas. And when Nick learns something interesting about how words are created, suddenly he's got the inspiration for his greatest plan ever . . .

Who says a pen has to be called a pen? Why not call it a *frindle?* Things begin innocently enough as Nick gets his friends to use the new word. Then, other people start calling a pen a frindle. Soon, the whole school is in uproar, and Nick has become the kids' hero and the bane of the teachers' lives. What can anyone do? Frindle doesn't belong to Nick anymore. The new word is spreading across the country, and there's nothing Nick can do to stop it.

ISBN 0 689 83658 9

The School Story

by Andrew Clements

Twelve-year-old Natalie Nelson is writing an amazing story about school life called *The Cheater*. Her best friend Zoe reckons it's brilliant – it should be a breeze to get it published, especially since Natalie's mum is an editor for one of the biggest publishing houses around.

While Natalie knows better, and doesn't want any special favours, Zoe won't take no for an answer. She concocts a stupendous scheme to get *The Cheater* into print. First, Natalie must come up with a cool pen-name for herself so her mum won't know it's her. Then Zoe will invent a literary agency and appoint herself its star agent to sell Natalie's book. By sticking at it, sticking together – and with the help of a supportive but weary teacher – it's a daring scheme that might just work...

ISBN 0 689 83717 8

Zagwitz
the Thingummagadgetician

Welcome to the thingummagadgetal
better known as Zagwitz – a potty, b
tor.

Zagwitz has transported himself a
twins Lucy and William, to the W
the Galaxy of Ideas. But the evil E
World of Creativity, plunging ev
squidginess forever.

Thankfully Zagwitz has a lot of str
of crackpot inventions on his side.
roller coaster ride of action, advent
Zag sets out to blast Eraser from hi

ISBN 07434 44020X